BARBARA BOTTNER

New York

For my brother, Jeffrey

{Imprint}
MAKE YOUR MARK

A part of Macmillan Publishing Group, LLC
120 Broadway, New York, NY 10271

Library of Congress Cataloging-in-Publication Data is available.

ISBN 978-1-250-20769-2 (hardcover) / ISBN 978-1-250-20770-8 (ebook)

Our books may be purchased in bulk for promotional, educational, or business use.
Please contact your local bookseller or the Macmillan Corporate and Premium Sales Department
at (800) 221-7945 ext. 5442 or by email at MacmillanSpecialMarkets@macmillan.com.

Book design by Elynn Cohen
Imprint logo designed by Amanda Spielman

First edition, 2020

1   3   5   7   9   10   8   6   4   2

fiercereads.com

You love this book: aye, okay!
But do not hide this work away.
Read it 'til your eyes turn blue
but when you're done, say adieu!

Avoid the book curse,
don't stumble and fall
thieves, of course, are unfit to know.
Share this book!
Off you go.

You can't trust Life to give you decent parents
or beautiful eyes, a fine French accent or an outstanding
flair for fashion. No, Life does what it wants.
It's sneaky as a thief. People themselves are sneaky.
I am sneaky. I'm also a thief. Looking back at
this last year, that's the lesson I learned.

Bronx, 1960

WHAT'S GOING DOWN

Richie O'Neill signals me from his apartment,
which is directly opposite mine.
He's waving his dad's Fulton GI flashlight,
describing tight circles that beam
directly into my bedroom window,
hissing alert:
Something important is going down.
Just knowing he's there, that I'm not alone,
helps me get through
so many days and nights.
All I have to do is peek around
the ugly purple thrift store curtains
my mother hung.
Even though she loves to sew,
she decorated my room
with "feel bad about yourself" drapes.
Thanks, Mom. I do.

LANDING GEAR

Richie and I have a system:
Horizontal swipes mean
come down to the lobby when you can.
But extensive, sweeping circles,
like you might see on a tarmac
when a plane's lost its landing gear,
mean emergency. Help. Five-star alarm.
(I lost my landing gear a long time ago.)

I open then close my curtains,
signaling my departure.
Then I grab my jacket;
the lobby's always cold,
except in summer,
when you wish to the Gods of the Bronx
that it would cool off.
But there are no gods
here in the Bronx.

MARRIED PEOPLE

Richie and I both have parents
who could compete to be
the most unhappily married people
in all of Parkchester.
The most destructive, too.
All of them thought that
moving into this vast, planned complex
of buildings—
designed to be a retreat
from the noisy urban streets—
would make life easier.
It's pretty nice here;
terra-cotta figurines
decorate the tall brick buildings.
There are oak, sycamore, and maple trees.
And we have parks, baseball fields, playgrounds.
Apartments have decent kitchens,
good carpeting, sunlight.
But, still, the city invades.
Ambulances, fire trucks, burglar alarms
shriek through the neighborhood.
Lumbering buses, kids cracking bats
against hardballs, street fights,
loud radios blasting sports scores,
girlfriends' singsong scolding
their no-good boyfriends—"*chico malo*"—
zip around us at all hours.
Nobody who lives in the Bronx can relax.

WHEN YOU'RE FOURTEEN

It's the night before the first day
of high school.
I was hoping, for once,
to be consumed with choosing an outfit.
Like a normal kid.
Entrances are everything
when you're my age.
Sometimes my father,
the globe-trotting Perfume Magnate,
the proud self-made man,
gives me the once-over.
He looks at me as if I'm a possible model
for a new scent he's launching
from his boutique company.
He says, coolly, "You're pretty."
I wait. It's never that simple.
"Not the prettiest," he usually clarifies.
According to him, this is a good thing
because, he says,
the ultra-gorgeous ones,
like Merilee Stabiner and Jessica Levin,
never bother to develop a personality.
It's creepy to me that he has these opinions
about girls my age.
That he's obsessed with beauty.
"But, Dad, my personality is problematic,"
I object at those times.
We both know *problematic*
is a guidance counselor word.
My mother calls me worse things.
I say,
"My so-called personality is too big

for this house.
Too big for my mother.
And sometimes for *me*, too."
He nods.
At least my father talks to me.

ONGOING WAR

So tonight, instead of concentrating
on questions like should I wear
a pleated skirt or a pencil-thin straight one,
a coral sweater or a blue-green one,
I'm descending in the elevator, deciding
if I should tell Richie how things are going
before or after
I hear *his* tale of woe.
Should I pretend
that, with his flashlight, he interrupted
only my clothing showdown?
This would be a lie.
I happened to see
his signal.
It reached all the way into our kitchen,
where I was hiding out,
trying to ignore the mayhem
coming from my parents' bedroom.
Rat-a-tat phrases were firing
from both sides of the ongoing war.
There might as well be gunfire,
might as well be blood seeping out
from under their door.
These angry nights
are more and more frequent.

EBONY PENCIL

Lucky for me, I like to draw,
which is why I was stationed
at the kitchen table,
furiously scratching a newsprint pad.
Newsprint is cheap.
You can make mistakes, experiment.
I was using my ebony pencil.
Once I really concentrate,
I can escape, lose track of time.
Obliterate sounds.
Take a vacation from the hostilities.
I was studying the geography of my gym socks,
determined to understand
why each sock has creases
that fall a certain way.
And the small mountains and shadows
that make it seem
like it is its own country.
It's more complicated than I thought!
This everyday white cotton sock
that I've folded hundreds of times
becomes fascinating! Compelling!
I'm shading, erasing, trying to get it right.
Loving every minute.
Drawing calms me down.

PROBABLY JAMES JOYCE

I shoved the pad under my bed,
rushed to the hallway.
The elevator—belching from its old motor
and stinking of macaroni and cheese,
cigarette butts, stale beer—finally arrived.
There are bits of old pizza crusts on the floor.
A cheap-looking magenta lipstick
lies missing its cap in the corner
like a reminder of someone's forced smile.
In the lobby, the door creaks open.
Richie's sitting on a bench reading.
He always has a book.
Probably James Joyce.
He's obsessed.

Then, there's arguing from across the street.
Richie slaps closed his paperback
when he sees me.
Some guy is yelling:
"Get your hands off me!
I'm a *Vietnam vet*, assholes!"
"That's my father!" Richie sputters.
"Can you believe this is his life, Maisie?
He was awarded the goddamn Bronze Star."
Everybody knows that Brian O'Neill
came back a hero
after he was injured in the war.
"He was one of the very first
sent to fight the Viet Cong,"
Richie says mournfully.
"Now he has night sweats.
He wakes up shouting!

My sister, Rebecca, gets freaked."
Richie omits
that his dad goes on drunken rampages.
I say, "I know, Richie.
I just wish he didn't take his demons
out on you."
Together, we race to the lobby entrance,
push open the heavy door.
"*Cocksuckers!*" screams Mr. O'Neill
a few yards away from us.
Two men forcefully shove him
against a police car. Richie goes pale.
"Cocksuckers!" screams Mr. O'Neill again.
"Asshole!" shout the cops.
There's scuffling. Yelps.
Mr. O'Neill's being arrested.
Again.
"I had to call the police.
He was going after Regina,"
Richie explains all raspy.
"Well, you can't have him
hurting your little sister."
But I realize that to throw
your dad in jail overnight
must be humiliating.

PASTEL PAINTING

"It makes everything worse,"
he agrees.
Richie almost never discusses his mother,
Caitlyn O'Neill.
If she were a painting, she'd be pastel.
It's like her outline is blurred.
She floats like a Chagall.
A beautiful Irish Chagall.
If I painted her,
I'd draw her in a dark pencil,
making heavy Braque outlines
so you could see her more clearly,
bring her back down to Earth,
down to her life here in the Bronx
so she could help her children.
Lustrous green eyes,
thin, elegant face.
A person you'd probably see every day
walking the streets of Dublin.
I'd make her into a formidable presence.
Someone who could hold the family together.
Because Richie's dad is a dish-flinger,
a wall-puncher.
I wonder if they have any plates
left to eat off in that doomed apartment.
Or if there's a draft in every room,
a wind blowing through every wounded wall.

LIKE FIRST COUSINS

Richie and I've known each other
since I was in kindergarten
and he was in third grade.
Back then, I didn't pay much attention to him.
But lately, for the last two years,
we're like cousins;
comparing notes about his dad
and my mom.
Sometimes we imagine
putting them in the ring
in Madison Square Garden
and selling tickets.
It would be a long fight,
but we think we'd make millions.
In the Bronx, we love a good battle
in the boxing ring, on TV, or in the streets.

Tomorrow or the next day,
Richie and I will sit together
and mumble our sad stories.

CARTOON FACE

"Will you be in school?" I ask.
"Of course," says Richie.
"Senior year! I have to get into college.
Or I'll end up like my dad."
"You'll never end up like him," I say.
"He has all that body hair. And a mustache."
I take a pencil out of my pocket
and sketch a cartoon

of Mr. O'Neill's face.
"I can't believe you can *do* that!"
says Richie.
I push the elevator button.
"See you tomorrow."
He tugs my sleeve.
"Take this!" he says. "But don't open it until later."
He hands me a plain white envelope.
"What is it?"
"It's nuthin'. Honestly. Nuthin' at all."

THUD

Upstairs, from the hallway,
I hear my brother, Davy,
eleven, playing the piano.
Well, it's more like plinking.
He has mad love for George Gershwin.
He bangs out chords from
An American in Paris almost every night.
But it gets quiet.
He must be reading the composer's bio.
He's consumed by both Gershwin boys.
I love that they're Jewish.
But Davy doesn't care about that.
Every note speaks to him.
I hotfoot it inside
to dry the last few dinner dishes.
Davy gets up from the piano bench.
"I can't wait to get out of this place,"
he says.
"Which place?" I ask. "This apartment?
The Bronx?"

"Yes," he says, and trudges off to his room.
He has no desire to talk to me.
I sit back down at my sketch pad
and try to master rendering the tiny stitches
on the heels of my socks
when I hear something thud.
It comes from my parents' bedroom.
Whatever it is,
it rolls and crashes.
I watch my pencil fall
in slow motion onto the floor.
I put my drawing pad down.
Their fights tighten my stomach,
make me grip my toes.
I forget to breathe.
I wonder: Maybe the police
should visit our apartment
after they finish with Mr. O'Neill.
I get my brother.
"Come on, Davy, let's watch TV," I say.
It's how we cope on nights like this.
I turn it on, volume high.
Davy slumps down next to me, and we sink down
into the overstuffed turquoise couch,
wanting to disappear.
For this brief moment Davy and I
are on the same side of the family war.

KIDS VERSUS PARENTS

My mother doesn't strike Davy.
Not once. Never. Ever.
He's safe.
I get jealous of that.
I am aligned with my dad.
At least he's not a slapper.
My grandma says I look like him.
I have my dad's brio, his boldness,
and not in a good way.
I'm his favorite,
but being his favorite doesn't help.
Lately, on fight nights,
instead of me and my dad
versus Davy and Judith,
it's kids versus parents.
Now Davy grabs my filthy
black pencil–marked hand
as if we're pals.
"It's okay, kid," I say.
We both know that's a lie.
But what's the big deal?
It won't kill me
to be nice to him,
older-sister style.

A HIT MAN?

Through the wall, Dad's hollering,
"You're nuts, Judith!
You need professional help!"
My mother uses the *bastard* word
a trillion times.
I picture her staring at Dad with her one good eye.
The blind one drifts and sees nothing.
It's scary if you don't know she has no vision in it.
And we didn't know this for a long time.
Now something else slams
against the wall, shatters.
I'm not sure if it's a chair
or someone's head.
This goes on and on,
from the beginning of
The Danny Thomas Show
to the end of *The Adventures of Ozzie and Harriet.*
When my parents are like this,
all I have is my brother.

When I'm this close to him,
I remember how innocent he smells.
He was born easygoing and benign,
unlike me, who, they claim,
came out yowling and cursing
like an Italian mafioso.
My mother says I'm still like that.
Like what? A *hit* man?
But I've heard my dad say,
"*You're* the crazy one, Judith!"
Once I overheard my grandmother tell her sister, my great-aunt
Dalvinka,

I was a difficult baby.
Why do I have to know this?
As if right from the start
I wanted to cause trouble?
I asked my gran,
"If a mother blames her newborn
for being colicky,
should she be a mother
in the first place?"
She answered me in Hungarian.
A language she knows I don't understand.

TOO YOUNG

Davy and I never talk much.
Even now, no words.
Anyway, I don't want to scare him.
I'm wondering,
maybe I should call my gran.
Joe and Judith have never thrown things
at each other before.
But Judith would kill me,
I mean kill me *dead*
for letting *her* mother know the truth.
I'm only fourteen and three quarters.
Way too young
and too annoyed to die.

BUZZ. BUZZ.

Finally, my parents are speaking
in normal tones, mumble, mumble.
I call this lull "the bargaining phase."
They bought a book that tells them
they must learn to de-escalate.
Once I snuck a peek at it.
I guess it works, at least once in a while.
The house is quiet now,
and Davy's eyes flutter closed.
He has a talent for shutting down.
He's a human turtle.
Dozing, he's drooling a little foamy river
down his flannel shirt.
I guess I glaze over, too,
because when my bleary eyes
open again,
the national anthem is playing on TV,
and there's a photo montage of the flag
and the station ID.
That means broadcasting is ending for the night.
This is followed by
black-and-white mind-numbing test patterns
that probably aren't that different
than what's going on in my brain.
Buzz. Buzz.

I feel like I reside on a battlefield.
Like the German painter George Grosz,
who survived WWI
And the artists Käthe Kollwitz, Oskar Kokoschka.
From their canvases and drawings,

I've learned something about
what they lived through.
I wish they could see *my* life.
Not nearly as difficult as theirs.
But maybe they could give me some tips.

STICK AROUND

Footsteps. My dad, buttoning up
his expensive cashmere overcoat,
bursts out of their bedroom
and rushes by us.
"Maisie, Davy,
I won't see you for a few days.
Leaving for a business trip."
He's like a firefly lately,
here, gone, here, gone,
and, like a firefly,
he lights up the place in tiny, short spurts.
"Hey, kids, don't look so forlorn!"
He winks.
"I'll be back. Don't worry!"
That wink is almost the worst part.
It's saying everything is okay.
But everything is not okay.
I jump up, mutely tug
his soft, creamy sleeve,
because the words "don't go!"
are glued in my throat
as if I swallowed a jar
of sticky peanut butter.
I want to say, "Dad, tomorrow's

the first day of high school!
Don't make me slink in there
all sad and distracted.
Stick around.
Ask me some questions, like
'Maisie, honey, do you have
all your textbooks?
Will any kids from last year
be in your class?
Are you worried about being in the AP?
Do you have art courses?
I sure hope so!'
You could say something encouraging,
like *'Maisie, you're the best.*
You have nothing to worry about.
The other kids would be lucky
to have you as a friend.'"
But no, the front door slams.
"Bye, Dad . . . love you too . . . coward!"
Coward because you're leaving
Davy and me with someone
you can't handle!
It's a good thing parents don't get report cards.

LAST YEAR

"I wonder how long he'll be MIA this time?"
I whisper to Davy. "Where does he go?
Last year he went to France.
Never even told us!"
"Paris!" he says, waking up. "I hope the bastard
never comes back."
"Are you kidding, Davy? *She's* the real problem."

"Not my problem, Maisie,"
he whispers, nodding off again.
I lead him to his sparrow-blue room
and manage to foist him
on top of his stupid truck-patterned bedspread,
wrestle off his smelly sneakers.
Asleep, he's almost purring like a kitten.
Asleep, I don't resent him at all.

BASKET CASE

Outside, the police have quit shouting
into their walkie-talkies.
The squad car,
with Mr. O'Neill inside,
finally screeches away.
Another one pulls up,
but after a brief conference,
it leaves also.
I watch until I'm pretty sure
the big show is over.
No signal from Richie,
so I climb into bed, fix the covers
how I like them, close my eyes.
I really want to fall asleep.

Last spring I was glum after Leslie,
my best friend, moved away midsemester.
Glum is not the word:
I was a basket case.
My grades plunged.
My drawings got weird,
as in ugly and tormented,

difficult to look at—even for me.
Drawings never lie.

WHO TO BE?

12:13 A.M. School starts at 9 A.M.
I have to figure out who to be.
Someone different than last year.
Smarter, cooler, and, despite my braces,
mysterious.
Good luck with that, Maisie!
You can't be mysterious
with all that hardware,
all those rubber bands in your mouth;
you might as well have
railroad tracks in there.
Choo choo.
Where's my train heading?
Nowhere.
I examine the outfits I've pulled out,
lying on my bed in silent competition.
I'm not in the mood for high school.
I'm not in the mood for anything.

ORIGINS OF LIFE

Now a sliver of moonlight hits
the paisley patterns
on the wallpaper in my room.
Amoeba-like shapes with colorful flourishes
remind me of biology, where we learn
about the origins of life.
When it all began.
A primitive period before time
that was microscopic and lively,
evolving over billions of years
into the world as we know it,
before there were humans
who yell and scream
over imaginary crimes.
This perception that I'm only one tiny,
unimportant nano-event
in human history comforts me.
I tell myself
we're all the same, basically.
Connected, even when it doesn't feel that way.
The wallpaper's the last thing
I see at night.
Mornings, I stare at it again
as my mother reads the charges
accumulated against me
while I was asleep.
(I'm always guilty of something.)
This family has taught me
to live high on adrenaline,
the way people do in a conflict zone.
That's how life is
inside a totalitarian system.

BANG. BANG. BANG.

In his bedroom, Davy, awake again,
knocks his head against his wall.
I have to admit, he's too distraught
for someone who still doesn't have
one single hair growing out
of his baby face.
Bang. Bang. Bang.
He's a human metronome.
Once he said, "I do it to escape the chaos
of this place."
"Why don't you just play some Gershwin?"
I asked.
He didn't bother to answer.

Judith made him pick out his carpet.
I remember how insistent she was
that he choose it for himself.
As if that could make him feel
that he belongs in a family of people
who have olive skin, greenish eyes
in common but mainly are falling apart.
Not falling, no. Ripping.
I wonder,
can you exchange one sort of hurt
for another?

THUMP, THUMP, THUMP

Mother marches into his room,
says: "Stop this!
It can't be good for you, David!
I worry about you."
She never speaks in a soft, concerned voice,
Why are you doing this, honey?
What's the matter?
Davy has an entire repertoire
for this habit.
He quits just long enough
for her to leave.
Then *bang. Bang. Bang* again.
It stops. I can't make out anything else.
Did she go back in?
Is she hugging him?
Straightening out his blankets?
Her few moments of maternal instinct
for the entire week are spent now.
And as soon as she leaves again,
thump, thump, thump:
a perfect rhythm.
It's distracting.
I can forget about it for a little while,
but then I can't doze off,
thump, thump.
He's not a boy,
he's a machine.
I tap the wall between us.
"Davy, *stop* it!"
He misses a thump.
Then another.

"Thank you! Go to sleep!"
But he begins again.
"That's bad for you, Davy!"
I hear those words as if I didn't say them.
It is bad for him, really bad.

SAYING "SISTER"

I get up, trot to his door, knock softly.
"Davy, please listen to your sister."
Saying "sister" somehow makes me
well up with tears.
And then I'm begging:
"Hey, Davy, open the door!"
It does open, slowly.
I notice his glassy eyes,
as if he's in a trance.
He goes back to bed.
He lets me take his warm, toasty hand.
It hits me:
Davy's hurting and fragile.
I wait while his eyes drift close.
I hear his soft breathing.
I can't believe
I never thought about this.
My brother is another me.

GARGOYLE

In my room again
I grab some socks for my cold toes,
crawl farther under the covers.
Sleep begins to brush my eyes.
But Judith barges through my door,
toppling the chair I'd leaned against it,
and flips on the overhead light.
She might as well be snorting fire.
"Where are my glasses, Maisie?"
I get up, stumble around, stub my toe,
don't see her glasses,
because they're never
in my room.
Meanwhile, on my small desk,
she spots my latest sketchbook.
She knows I'm always drawing,
knows my eyes are greedy
to see and to learn.
"These pathetic scratches
make you think you have enough talent
to become an artist?"
She laughs.
I answer, "Grandmother knits.
You, Mother, sew.
Creativity runs in the family."
She flips it to my newest pages, snorts.
"Creativity? That's what you call this?
What's it supposed to be?"
"A sock," I mumble.
"A sock? A *sock*?"
She tears up my sketch into small

newsprint flakes that float over my carpet.
"There's your creativity!"
Now I only feel rage at her.
This feeling is uncomplicated.
Uncomfortable, but uncomplicated.
It's like poison.
What did I ever do to her?

THE QUEEN OF SOMETHING

"These fights between
me and your dad are your fault!
You know that, right?"
I should keep my big mouth shut;
nothing good will come out of it.
But it opens:
"I do know that, Mother.
Everything's always my fault.
Including that Davy bangs his head
every night.
He'd rather do that
than think about our family.
And that's because of me?"
She snorts, leaves to go,
probably to her sewing machine,
even at this late hour.
There's always some stupid evening gown
she's designing like she's the queen
of something in her mind.

WHACKED

Heart racing, I gather up my sketch fragments,
dump them, then return to bed,
thinking how, like most babies,
I must have been born ready,
yearning for life.
Until I was whacked
on my newborn behind.
I must have obliged
with a terrifying shriek,
because at that moment,
things fell apart between us.
I'm trouble for my mother;
my mother's trouble for me.

REPAIR

Head on my pillow,
I remember Richie's white envelope
from before.
"Before" seems like lifetimes ago.
I'm too tired to read it.
I remember the first note he gave me
in the fifth grade.
That one was something about
some book he liked.
I should have known!
It was about James Joyce,
naturally!
I think, no matter what,
it's easier to be a boy.
All Richie has to do for school

is comb his reddish-blond hair.
He has a white complexion, slim body,
and a look on his face that says
do not touch!
It keeps people guessing.
I toss around, unable to give in to sleep
though I crave it.
I argue, plead with my brain:
Stop chattering!
Pure exhaustion eventually takes over.
I descend into the catacombs of unconsciousness.

SMILE A LITTLE

Later, at 7 A.M.,
the sun blasts through my window,
the most jubilant of friends.
Despite last night,
the miracle happens again:
I can somehow face the day.
I get close to the mirror.
My ears are too large,
my breasts are teeny.
My hair just looks depressed,
and where does my nose
think it's going?
I check for food stuck in my braces,
always a potential embarrassment.
The only positive development:
My eyelashes are getting thicker.
And my skirt seems kind of short.
Does that mean maybe
my legs are getting longer?

Judith peeks in, catches me looking.
"Don't fall in love with yourself.
I was better looking
when I was fourteen and a half."
"I know you were *beautiful*, Mom."
This sentence always pacifies her.
It happens to be true.
My mother was stunning.
But I wish I could ask her,
"Mom, how could I be in love with myself
when no one else is in love with me?'

GIRLS NAMED TIFFANY

I'm wearing my plaid navy-and-ochre
shirtwaist dress.
My brown eyes pop from the color contrast.
I refuse to wear bright shades,
like pink or periwinkle.
"Periwinkle" even sounds idiotic.
It's good for girls named Tiffany
with moms who say "I love you"
every other minute.
I have a lot of opinions
when it comes to colors.
Leslie was the one with the great complexion,
blond, blue-eyed,
she just couldn't wear purple.
Which *I* discovered!
Whenever I'm worried,
I close my eyes
and mix paints in my head.

COME ON!

Davy's sitting at the kitchen table.
Mother's in her silk robe, making breakfast.
"What do you want to eat?"
she grumbles.
Davy's shirt is rumpled,
his shoelaces aren't tied,
and his hair is sticking straight up.
I wet it down for him,
but he wriggles away.
"Stop fussing over me, Maisie!"
He tackles his scrambled eggs.
When she's in the picture,
all alliances are officially suspended.

When Davy and I get to the door
with our book bags,
my mother opens it, smiles.
"You two!"
She looks at us almost tenderly.
Longing rises up my spine,
a hungry snake.
It threatens to make me
feel something moronic:
a belief that affection could be
just around the corner.
I know better than to allow
that brief glimmer of kindness to mean anything.
It could undo me.
I say gruffly,
"Davy. Put on your scarf already!
Come on!"

Davy hugs her.
We ride to the lobby silently.
Then we tumble out
into the brisk Bronx morning
without a word between us.

HUNGRY LOOKS

I form a plan.
On the way to school
I'll drop the unloved me
like an ill-fitting garment
and embrace the other, bold, sassy me,
who sneaks a new mascara wand
from her pocket, who jokes and flirts,
arches her back because she loves it
when boys get those yearning looks
on their nerdy, awkward baby faces.
They're full of devilish wonder to me.
Even Richie sometimes radiates that magic.

ROSY RED CHEEKS

Outside, the furious September wind blasts
as if it means to banish the leaves,
newspapers, soda cans, and detritus everywhere.
I hope it gives me rosy red cheeks, bright eyes!
Davy and I walk together
until we get to his school, PS 106.
"Don't watch me leave.
I'm not a baby!"
he says and trundles inside.

* * *

Farther on, my high school's jumping!
Outside, there's first-day-of-the-year excitement.
You can almost see hormones
leaping off people,
making them behave like nervous mosquitoes.
Some are smoking, some giggling.
The cool kids hold back, watching.
The pretty girls look one another over
as if they're judging
a Miss America contest.

GYM

The gym is crowded and hot,
steam rising out of the radiators
like a dying volcano.
It already stinks like a basketball game,
and it's not even 9 A.M. yet.
There are some familiar faces
and ones I've never seen before.
What's important right now is
will any boys look my way?
Or will they pretend I don't exist?
And if they pretend I don't exist,
is it because they like me,
or is it because
I really *don't* exist for them?
Maybe if my mother didn't
spit out my name like a curse
and my father didn't use our front door
like the turnstile in the IRT,

the opposite sex wouldn't seem so intriguing
and so absolutely necessary.

BUT CRAZY

It was Leslie who said
I had an unnatural hunger
for male attention,
the way some girls have for chocolate
or new clothes or ballet class.
She even said I was famished!
I couldn't argue.
I've been this way for as long
as I can remember.
I'm not proud of it, but it's the truth.
In the sixth grade I made up a game.
I flirted with every single boy.
As soon as they began
to follow me around,
I brushed them off.
I didn't miss a one.
I knew it was over the top.
But it was fun. But too much.
Still, it made me feel extra alive.
I've studied magazines,
learned how to smile a certain way
sort of like a Cheshire Cat.
It magnetizes boys.
My little secret.

GENIUS

We're waiting
to go to homeroom.
This year I'm in the AP.
Advanced Placement.
We're the brilliant ones.
Richie O'Neill, wearing a cobalt shirt
that sets off his smoky blue eyes,
finally wanders in
and folds into the seat next to me,
staring down at his scuffed shoes.
I guess he could be handsome
if he didn't look as if an alien
was siphoning off his energy
like in a sci-fi story by Isaac Asimov.
Just because Richie is Irish
and his family doesn't have much money,
doesn't mean he isn't whip smart,
because he is.
I've known that since elementary school
at PS 106 on St. Raymond's Avenue.
He was the most famous third-grader;
we even heard about him in kindergarten.
He had a teacher, Mrs. Sanbloom,
who famously didn't wear a bra,
who drew a grid on the blackboard,
said, "Connect all the dots."
Not one person could do it.
Richie was the only one
who realized that you could connect those dots
only by going *outside* the grid.
Until then, nobody expected
Richie to be the genius in the bunch.

OLD BEACH HOUSE

I still have the letter Richie gave me.
Does he expect me to say something?
Here in Parkchester,
the Irish have an attitude about Jews.
Richie's not like that.
"Oops, didn't open your envelope yet,"
I whisper to him.
His cellophane skin blushes.
"No problem."
Richie rolls up his sleeve
to just above the elbow.
Twin purple bruises blaze on his arm.
I hike up my sleeve.
Our bruises have a silent,
eerie conversation.
Then with perfect timing,
we pull our sleeves down.
He opens his notebook,
briefly looks up, shrugs, then ignores me.
He gets this way sometimes,
shuttered up like an old beach house
that hasn't been used for years.

WISE GUY

The bell rings.
We're off to our homerooms.
Inevitably my big ears, small breasts
will slink inside,
find a seat in the second row.
As we shuffle through the hallways,
the principal welcomes us
over the intercom.
I warn myself: Do *not* be a wise guy
on the first day of school, Maisie!
Because if you're going to be a wise guy,
you shouldn't look all knock-kneed and weird.
You have to be like Nancy O'Malley:
cheerleader-cute; straight, white,
slightly buck teeth; oozing confidence
like she's leader of the free world.
Or Florence de La Cruz: breasts;
heavy-lidded movie-star eyes;
a sexy mole near her upper lip;
and so much shiny hair,
like a Clairol model
whose life will be a dream
even though she comes from the Bronx.
Merilee Stabiner and Jessica Levin
huddle together, naturally.
Both have ponytails,
perfect profiles, new clothes.
I bet their apartments are like a TV sitcom.
No slamming doors . . . or hot rage . . .

FOCUS!

Focus, Maisie!
Find an actual friend!
You need one since your bestie
moved to Long Island.
Lucky Leslie Loeb,
two-story house,
lush green lawn, motorboat, fast car,
climbing up the social ladder
in her brand-new patent leather flats.
I miss her.
I call her Leslie of Long Island now.
I write her, but lately she hardly writes back.
Maisie, I remind myself,
come back to this moment.
Do *not* get kicked out of class
or called into the principal's office
like last year.
Do not get how you get when you hurt inside.
So out comes that phony
jack-in-the-box personality
that blurts out things you imagine are hilarious
(and generally aren't).

I LOVE LUCY–FUNNY

My teacher, Miss Morgan—
Matisse-blue eyes,
Renoir-pink cheeks, pretty,
and not just Bronx pretty, either—
takes attendance.
When she calls his name,
Nathan Trialas whistles,
says "Kiss my ass"
under his breath.
I say "Kiss my tonsils"
with my mouth clamped shut,
so it comes out a Jimmy Durante whisper.
I'm out of control and it's only 9:30!

The girl next to me
slaps her hand on the desk, cracking up.
It wasn't that funny.
I sure hope Miss Morgan didn't hear.
Mercifully, she keeps taking roll.
The girl, kind face with sly,
witty eyes, and curly, dark hair
springing off her head in all directions,
is giving me the thumbs-up
and still giggling,
like I'm *I Love Lucy*–funny.

ROMANTIC

Over lunch—institutional lasagna,
cardboard noodles, gray meat—
I find out her name is Rachel.
She says Mrs. Noble,
who was supposed to be
our homeroom teacher,
was already married when she fell in love
with Mr. Zeitler and ran off with him.
Isn't that romantic?
And terrible, of course, awful!
We sit there dreamily,
imagining the drama in our midst.
I love that two chunky,
middle-aged teachers,
who wore wrinkled clothes
and scuffed shoes,
were having amorous interludes
that disrupted so many lives
because of their passionate love.
"I'm thinking," says Rachel,
"that they went to Bali."
"From Bronx to Bali," I say
in a radio announcer's voice.
I suddenly realize:
"Before summer break,
Mrs. Noble had been getting dolled up."
"I noticed that, too!
But can you imagine feeling lust
for Mr. Zeitler?" asks Rachel.
"I remember him," I say.
"He was shy, had light-brownish fuzz

on his upper lip.
He often hummed show tunes in class.
His big curious eyes rested on us
as if *we* had the answer to something.
I loved him for that."
"Me too!"
Her toothy smile is like
the bright headlights of a car.

NOT THE TUBA

"I hope when I feel lust,"
says Rachel,
"it's with someone cute and sexy.
Maybe a musician."
I admit: "I already feel lust.
Sometimes it happens
in the middle of doing homework.
Very uncomfortable!
Or sometimes when I'm doing nothing,
a fire rises inside of my solar plexus.
It happens a lot!"
"Wow!" says Rachel. "You're so honest!"
Even if I wanted to stop,
the words just keep bursting out.
"And when I see myself naked,
I imagine someone else
seeing me that way.
Touching me, looking into my eyes,
murmuring all kinds of sexy things.
I kiss myself in the mirror
and end up having to take a shower."

I look at this girl I just met,
thinking what an idiot I am
to spill out these secrets.
"Maisie, you're one hot tamale!"
She laughs.
"What instrument would your musician play?"
I ask, trying to return to
a safe conversation.
"Me?" asks Rachel.
"I can hardly think after what you just said."
"Don't you feel lust, Rachel?"
She's quiet.
"Well, I wouldn't want a tuba player,"
she says finally.
"That wouldn't do it for me."
"Okay. No tuba players,"
I say, relieved.
"Accordion?"
She squeals, "No!"
I make a motion of crossing them off
an imaginary list.
She laughs.
So I'm thinking, this might not be
the worst year in human history.
High school might be my big break,
when I find a real girlfriend,
someone in this universe who gets me.

TEETH

Rachel and I have Language Arts
and Social Studies together!
I scribble notes during class,
but I also covertly sketch her
when she's not looking.
At lunch I open my notebook
to show her my drawings, blurt out:
"You have the best teeth!"
"Like teeth are a big beauty item?"
she asks.
"Large teeth *are* a beauty item!
Look in the magazines.
The best-looking people
have giant, oversize teeth."
"You're weird, Maisie.
What about my knees, huh?"
She tugs on her skirt.
"Did I ever show you these perfect knees?"
"Your knees are bony," I say.
"Shut up, Maisie."
"But, Rachel, you more than
make up for it with your *great teeth*."
"I'm a good chewer,"
she says drolly. "But you can really draw, Maisie.
I'm impressed!"
Good! I want her to be impressed.

THE WORLD SORT OF YAWNS

After school, Rachel and I walk home.
Richie appears and saunters behind us,
squishing dead leaves with his sad, old
but newly polished loafers.
A breeze wafts our hair,
birds flutter onto a branch together
and squawk about important matters.
In that moment, time stretches out
and the world sort of yawns,
and the dark cloud
that I take with me everywhere
drifts off.

PACK A DAY

Rachel tells me about her brothers,
Jake and Jonathan.
And she says casually,
"My mom is an oil painter."
"She must be amazing," I say,
wanting to jump up and down
on the street like a toddler getting a toy.
"I can't wait to meet her."
Rachel shrugs, says her mom, Kiki,
smokes a pack a day.
Acts too girlish, is kind of a hippy.
"Sounds good to me," I say.
"*Pas fantastique*, Maisie."
"You speak French?" I gasp.
Rachel explains that one summer,

when she was nine,
she lived in Toulouse.
Her father worked there as a journalist
after the war and likes to visit.
"Je parle Français un petit peu, aussi,"
I squeak.
"Fantastique, cherie!
Nous parleronsen Français ensemble,
n'est-ce pas?"
She sounds fluent
and has a convincing French accent.
Now I'm impressed.

PARCE QUE

Catching up, Richie O'Neill groans,
"Ooh la la!" Says, "That's all *I* learned
in French from Mrs. Moreau.
Elle m'embête. Elle est une monstre."
"She's a monster?" Rachel asks.
"But you pronounce French
so well, Richie!" I tease.
Richie turns crimson,
which makes him look handsome,
not even older-brother handsome.
Then he cuts out in front of us.
"He's cute!"
Rachel whispers.
"Boyfriend material?"
"Friends!" I say. "Friends only!"
I don't mention the reason
that Richie and I are bound together.
For a moment, I wish he and I

came from a crisp, normal family like Rachel's.
"Do you think maybe you could go for him?"
I ask.
"Me? No, no! I already have a crush,"
Rachel murmurs.
"I'm all ears."
"I am all not saying more."
She laughs, then invites me over.
In this nano-moment
comes an understanding:
Rachel and I are going to be
lifelong friends.
I can taste something sweet,
as if it were dessert.
I close my eyes and release Leslie Loeb.
I see her fly away into her new life.

WOUNDED

Rachel points to her building,
says "Au revoir," waves.
"À bientôt."
Richie waits for me.
We walk the rest of the way together,
discussing school, curricula,
the new kids, the best teachers.
Then Richie says, "You know our principal,
Mrs. Heffernan, is famous for running a tight ship.
When she defected from Erasmus Hall
in the means streets of Brooklyn
twenty-three years ago,
she brought the mean part *with* her to the Bronx.
So we can't be jerks, Maisie!"

"I don't do well
with female authority, Richie."
"You can't afford to cross Heffernan's
heavy-footed path," he warns.
"You mean I shouldn't say stuff like
'here comes the heifer'?"
"Troublemaker!" he says
with mock disgust.
I like amusing him.

BEAUTIFUL TENOR

Then, out of the blue, he stops walking
and blurts an entire paragraph:
"It's the war that did this to him.
In 1957, my dad was sent to Vietnam
working for MAAG
and the US Information Agency.
He and twelve guys were wounded
in bombings in Saigon.
Before he left, he used to tousle my hair
and toss the ball with me.
He sang Irish drinking songs.
Mostly he loved Tommy Makem."
"I never heard of him," I admit.
"You never heard of the Clancy Brothers?"
Richie starts singing:
"'As I was a goin' over the far-famed Kerry mountains,
I met with Captain Farrell and his money he was counting.
I first produced my pistol and I then produced my rapier,
saying "Stand and deliver" for he were a bold deceiver . . .'"
He's belting it out at the top of his lungs.

For some reason, I start laughing.
"Never mind. You're not Irish.
You wouldn't understand," he says.
"It was different then, that's all.
But when he returned,
something that had been part of him fell out.
He's never been the same.
I'm trying to understand."
I don't know what to say.
I'm sorry?
That sounds ridiculous.
I hate wars?
Not helpful.
"I remember your dad's beautiful tenor.
I'd lean out my window and listen!"
"Yeah," he says, "he has a great voice."
Then Richie tosses me a generic wave
and splits.
I wonder if this is what that paper
he gave me is about?

OF COURSE!

Mother, Davy, and I are having a
meatballs-and-spaghetti dinner
on our lime-tinted
formica kitchen table,
minus my father, of course.
We don't discuss him.
Or when he's coming back.
Or if.
Or where he went?

Which means every single minute that he's gone,
I'm tense.
To help ensure my survival,
I try to entertain Judith.
I tell her in dazzling detail
about our teachers' romance.
"So, Mom, where do you think
Mrs. Noble and Mr. Zeitler went?"
"To hell!" she says.
Of course!
She stands firmly against happiness,
as if it's a bad religion.

Davy helps her clean off the table.
Then I hear him playing the chords to
An American in Paris on the piano.
Mother hums along, or tries.
Her voice goes sharp, but even if it didn't,
it grates on me.
I can't blame Davy for playing it safe.
Being designated "the good one,"
the one who doesn't get smacked.

NOTEBOOK PAPER

In my bedroom, I figure
I should get around to reading
what Richie wrote me.
I open his lined notebook paper,
read his neat, self-conscious handwriting:
When I die, Dublin
will be written in my heart.
—James Joyce

What's *this* supposed to mean?
Is Dublin a substitute for the Bronx?
True, many Irish live here,
but there's nothing about this place
that would inscribe it in anyone's heart.
Our history is pedestrian,
except for Edgar Allan Poe.
And Woodlawn Cemetery
is a who's who of famous people:
Joseph Pulitzer, Herman Melville,
Fiorello LaGuardia,
except that most of them
didn't live in the Bronx.
They came here to rest in peace.
Personally, I believe if you can't find peace
when you're alive,
when you're dust it's probably too late.

IN CASE WHAT?

I signal Richie to meet me downstairs.
I fix my hair and dab eyeliner on.
Just in case.
"In case what, Maisie?"
I ask myself.
"In case Richie and you . . ."
But then my self shuts up completely.
Richie and I are *not* a thing!
I just love makeup!

In the lobby we go over
French phrases.
I complain to Richie

that the French don't really want anyone
to learn their language.
What's the point of giving every noun an article?
Why's a table feminine?
Why's a horse masculine?
What could that possibly add
to understanding or enriching anything?
"*Tu es drôle*," says Richie.
"I am not! I'm serious!"

MAD LOVE

"What did you mean
by that James Joyce quote?
Why this mad love for Dublin?"
I ask, hoping for more info.
He tells me Dublin's been around
since something or other BC.
It's near Neolithic burial tombs!
The Druids lived there.
There've been religious wars, rebellions.
It has cobbled streets, thirteenth-century castles,
rolling green hills that pitch into the Irish Sea.
"My dad told me that the people in the pubs
sing ballads that break your heart.
George Bernard Shaw, Oscar Wilde,
Jonathan Swift were born there.
It's the most beautiful place on Earth,"
he says.
"Except for Paris. Joyce lived there
while he wrote *Ulysses*.
One day I'll live abroad.
That's a promise."

Someone walks in front of us on their way
to the mailboxes. We grow silent.

"My dad's back home,"
Richie mumbles.
"He swears he's never drinking again!
I hope he means it this time!"
I nod, say I truly hope so, then add,
"I wish my mother could do something
to change.
But there's nothing she could do
to quit being herself."
"Well then, here's to alcoholics,"
says Richie.
"Hear, hear!" I say.
So, with fake feeling, I fake toast.

A CLUE?

"Richie, what about
'When I die, Dublin
will be written in my heart'?"
I can't shake the quote.
"God, I hope by the time I die,
a lot of other places
are written in *my* heart.
France. Bali. The Amazon rain forest.
I'm trying to live, not die, Richie."
"Me too," he says.
"Good! Do you believe we're all marked
by the place we're born?
That these streets and old buildings
will always stick with us

like a wad of gum
that's lost its flavor?
Or are you trying to teach me
about James Joyce?"
We're both silent as an old man
in a beret enters the lobby
and pushes the elevator button.
He smiles at us, revealing a gap
between his teeth.
In that moment, I picture him as a young boy.
I smile back.
Finally, the elevator comes and he hobbles inside.
"You gave that guy a reason
to keep on living," says Richie
with a lilt in his voice.

"I don't know much about Joyce," I say,
"except the famous Molly Bloom speech:
'. . . yes and his heart was going like mad
and yes I said yes I will Yes.'"
"Likely the sexiest lines ever written,"
says Richie.
How am I supposed to respond?
As long as we're just pals it doesn't matter.
But now, the way his eyes
land on me stirs me up.
Is he flirting?
Do I want him to flirt?
Or am I simply confusing him
with what Molly Bloom has made me feel?
When I look again, he's changed back
into my comfortable-as-a-worn-slipper
neighbor and pal. And I'm glad.

BOOKWORM

Without my dad's protective presence,
I have to be exquisitely wise, on alert,
to keep Judith from lashing out.
I pretend my classes are incredibly compelling.
I make sure she knows that ninth grade
in a new school's a lot to deal with.
When I foresee Judith's nostrils flaring,
eyebrows hooded, a storm brewing,
I fashion myself into a serious,
hunkered-down bookworm.
I even offer to read aloud to her
from our first novel assignment,
Animal Farm.
I garble phrases explaining the parable
of Marx and Stalin and the Russian Revolution
until my mother's eyes glaze over.
I study French verbs out loud,
je vais, il va, nous allons,
jump ahead just to confuse her:
the difference between
the imperfect, *j'allais,*
and the past perfect, *j'etais aller.*
She never learned any languages.
I talk about algebraic equations
as if "X equals what?"
were the three most
fascinating words in the world.

GLAD TO BE HOME

Two weeks later, while we're eating
liver and burned onions,
(my mother resents cooking),
my Paul Newman–handsome dad—
dressed in a fancy three-piece
Hart Schaffner Marx suit, silk tie, handkerchief,
slick hair, heavy aftershave—wafts inside,
as if he learned how to enter a room
from Frank Sinatra.
So smooth.
I expect him to open his mouth and croon.
Instead he sits next to me
while my mother gets a plate from the kitchen.
"Did you know in Italy,
men take mistresses?" he whispers,
as if we were in the middle of talking about movers,
shakers, and jet-setters,
which, I suppose technically,
my father is.
(He had his photo taken with Catherine Deneuve!
"She's the face of my new perfume,"
he explained.)
I shake my head.
"How would I know about mistresses?"
"It keeps the family together in the long run,"
he says enthusiastically.
"Are you telling me
about the long run of *our* family?"
"I'm just telling you how Europeans are, Maisie.
I thought you aspired to be sophisticated!
Europe's been around a long time," he says.
He's thinking ahead, into the future.
But I don't want to go there.

PEACHY KEEN

I only want to go backward,
or sideways into a TV show,
where everything is peachy keen,
where dads are not ladies' men
or playboys and never were.
Or if they were, it's in the distant past,
before they became adults with
bills and mortgages.
That's what I think about
when my too-good-looking dad,
reeking of aftershave,
returns from Italy.

At least, he says Italy is where he was.
"I'm glad to be home," he announces,
"but the plane ride was no fun;
storms over the Atlantic lasted for hours!"
He's taking off his coat, draping it on a chair
instead of hanging it up,
which, right off the bat, frosts Judith.

MADE IN ROME

But she controls herself and hangs it up.
From his upbeat conversation,
my dad has no idea
what it's like for us when he's gone.
What it's like for *me*.
This isn't the time to tell him,
so I sit on the plastic hassock
on the flokati rug as he unpacks.
He hands me an intricate
beaded black purse.
A masterpiece. To die for.
MADE IN ROME, the label says.
So maybe he did go to Italy.
"I wish you could have come with me,
kids," he says.
"The cities, oh, you'd love them.
The beauty! You, Maisie, as an artist,
you'd be even more transfixed
than I was and more knowledgeable."
I wonder, was he there with his mistress?
Why do I think he has a mistress?
"I bet you and Maisie would have a blast,"
says Davy,
"without me or Mother along."
"I wouldn't have a blast without you,
son," says my dad.
But my brother stomps off, muttering unintelligibly.

"The *David*, the frescoes, the architecture, the bridges!
Those famous hills outside of Florence,
the Ponte Vecchio, Roma, the Colosseum.

Not to mention the little local restaurants,
the *piccolo negozi*; street life's everywhere.
I have to take you back there
just to watch you go out of your mind!"

I wonder why, when he left,
he never mentioned this trip.
He's good at his business.
My mother never gives him any credit.
I don't understand that.
He has his own fragrance company!
His products are in all the stores!
Actresses say they love the scents.
He says his goal is to make enough money
to move us to Manhattan!

When he's right in front of me,
I want to tell him about Rachel,
Richie, Yossarian from *Catch-22*,
French class, art class.
Everything, I guess, about high school.
He says he wants to talk, too, but later.
Mother hates it when he wants to be with me,
so now there's deadly silence.
I smile. Dad smiles, too.
It's awful.

ITALIAN PERFUME

He hands me a postcard of the Uffizi Gallery.
He describes the art he saw.
He says he thinks I have talent!
And that I should see great paintings,
the masterpieces.
I feel close to him when he speaks like this
because, from his lively green eyes,
I believe he really means it.
But my skin prickles:
He probably should be saying
some of this to my mother.
I want to brag to her,
"See, Mom? Dad thinks of me, not you!
Why? Because you're a shrew!
Which is why he loves to talk to *me*.
Why he invites me places!"
Then I notice her face: incredibly downhearted.
I get an unusual pang for her.
I don't say my truth.
That never works out.

PLAYBOY

Instead, I slip my hand inside my new purse
to feel the fine silk lining.
Such luxury!
My fingers pull out a delicate lace hankie
with a pungent, sticky-sweet aroma,
smudged with rosy lipstick.
This makes me think of my grandma Ruth.
Sometimes, often, when she's sipping coffee,
she becomes gossipy.
She calls Joe "a good earner."
But after a glass or two of wine,
she claims, in her clotted Hungarian accent,
"Your farder, heez a ladyeez man.
A 'playing boy.'"
I correct her:
"You mean a 'playboy,' Gran?"
"Yes!" Then she quickly adds,
"But he has to be in his business."
She sneaks a glance at my mother.
I wonder what she'd say about the lipstick?
She'd say something, that's for sure.

TA-DA!

I show the evening bag to Judith.
But I'm already wondering,
who used this little beauty before me?
What does she look like?
Who is she?

Joe brings Davy into the living room.
For him, there's a tissue-soft leather wallet.
Davy discovers ten thousand Lira inside!
"Italian money looks so cool," he says.
"Pretty," my dad explains.
"Not worth much, but enjoy."
Davy tries to read the bills:
"Banca D'Italia . . ."
"Ta-da!" My dad presents my mother with perfume.
"Don't you 'ta-da' me," she says.
"You buy your daughter an evening bag,
but for me more perfume?
I bet it's a stupid sample!
You probably didn't even buy it, Joe!"
My father yells that the perfume
was more expensive than my bag.
And she should read the label.
It's not *his* brand, for Chrissake.
"Did you hear that, Davy?"
my mother says,
trying to get him on her side.
She hurls the bottle across the room.
It smashes and breaks.
Our house will reek for weeks
from the scent
of their bad marriage.

LOATHSOME VISITOR

I'm getting cramps!
They're growing more and more intense,
roiling my insides
as if I swallowed a typhoon.
There's a thick, gluey wetness
between my legs.
It's the loathsome "visitor."
Finally!
I'm nearly fifteen, way overdue!
Thick, warm, cherry-red blood
almost gushes out of me.
I open the drawer where my mother
keeps her sanitary pads,
stick one in my panties, and lie down.
Getting to be a woman
is a huge, life-changing moment.
You can't turn back.
The cramps are telling me
that I'm growing up
and that growing up isn't going to be—
OUCH!—any sort of picnic.

HUMAN FEMALES

I want an aspirin. Or a kiss, maybe.
Or wine, and I don't even like wine.
I hear my mother's shoes stomping toward me.
Could this moment be special,
simply about being human females?
Should I tell her?
No!
But then I'm on my feet,
running into the kitchen.
"It happened!" I blurt out.
"My period! It's happening right now!"
Her hand goes back and stings my cheek.
Thwap! Then again, the other cheek. *Thwap!*
"Don't look so stricken, Maisie," she says.
"My mother slapped me,
her mother slapped her.
It's good luck, a Hungarian tradition.
One day you will slap your daughter, too."
She phones her mother to tell her the news.
I wonder if this truly was a good-luck slap
or just another lucky chance to hit me.

SHE CAN REALLY DANCE

When the cramps finally quiet down,
I get up and decide
to listen to my favorite fast songs
on the Chubby Checker album.
I play the same track over and over,
play it loudly.
I'm twisting, and I'm shouting,
twisting on the outside

to match how twisted I feel on the inside.
I'm dancing, madly dancing
alone in my room for the longest time.
If you saw me from outside my window,
I bet you would think, *She can really dance.*
But what I'm mostly doing
is trying to feel the ground under my feet.

BITE INTO LIFE

The next day, as soon
as I get home from school
and walk into the apartment,
Judith starts in on me.
"I still have cramps," I mumble.
"So do I!" she says.
"The worst one is named Maisie!"

So I call Rachel,
ask her if I can bring over some rugelach.
"We have coffee cake!" she says.
She sings a little happy song.
"So hurry!"

As I walk toward her building,
I pass Richie sitting on a bench reading.
Nearby, kids are playing stickball.
One makes a hit.
The ball goes hurtling straight for Richie,
just missing his head.
None of the guys stop,
not even for a minute to wonder,
"Hey, are you shook up?"
None of them approach him.
Not one "sorry, man."

I wish Richie would stride over to the mound,
like his stocky, fierce dad might,
and warn them not to mess with him.
But he only turns around, stunned and dazed.
There are times, like now,
I worry that Richie,
unlike James Joyce,
doesn't want to bite into life.
I worry that if he did,
he'd spit life right out.

COLORED BOTTLES

A few blocks down,
I spot Rachel on the street.
She's waving goodbye to someone.
A boy! He's tall, walks with a swagger.
I can't see his face.
But something about him makes me want to.
When I get closer to Rachel, I ask,
"Is that the 'crush' guy?
Nice shoulders!"
"Gino has nice everything,"
she says suggestively,
adds a giggle I've never heard before.
I wonder what "everything" she means?
"He's a senior, too!
A senior, no less!"
She does a little twirl,
then points up to her building.
"Look up! Look at my mother's newest creation!"

Yellow, blue, red, purple bottles reflect
the last moments of the late-October sun

in one of Rachel's windows.
Who would ever think of displaying colored glass
to create an urban rainbow?

BLUE-AND-WHITE FLOORS

Inside, Rachel's kitchen
has blue-and-white linoleum floors,
like a checkerboard.
"The decor was my mom's idea.
Once we moved all the furniture
and played checkers sitting on the floor!"

Rachel's mom appears with coffee cake on a plate.
She has long jet-black hair;
wears loose, colorful, fringy clothes and
dangly earrings; and has eyes bigger even than her daughter's.
They're direct and clear.
Her graceful fingers have lots of silver rings,
and her skin is peachy and smooth.
A smile hovers over her face,
which makes me wonder—
what's she so happy about?
I realize she's finishing up a story about Mykonos.
"Of course we were all a little drunk at the time,"
Kiki laughs.
Rachel shrugs.

"You know us Greeks!" says Kiki.
"Always loving to have *fun!*"

Am I really inside a world where a grown-up talks to me
as if I'm actually a person
and not the bubonic plague?

NO SUBTITLES

Paintings are everywhere;
large, small, abstract, and colorful.
Rachel's house pulses with life:
jazz music plays on the stereo,
hanging beads separate the rooms and hallways,
lentil soup cooks on the stove,
and tie-dye languishes in the sink.
Very bohemian!
It makes me think
I've been living inside a sad black-and-white
Polish film with no subtitles,
no musical soundtrack.
"I love everything here," I gush.
"I love the art."
"Some are my paintings, some are Rache's,
and some are from our friends,"
says Kiki,
her eyes coated with emerald-green eye shadow.
"Are you an artist?"
"I scribble stuff," I say.
"She's good," brags Rachel.

At the kitchen table,
we eat off hand-painted plates.
Kiki asks me tough questions
like a private detective.
Rachel laughs, says, "Don't worry, Maisie,
Kiki always does this;
she worries that I'm going to bring
a criminal home.
I guess she doesn't trust me."

"Of course I trust you!" says Kiki.
"I'm just doing my job."

RICH HUSBANDS

"She's studying to be a shrink,"
Rachel explains.
"She never used to be like this
when she was a full-time painter."
"I was always like this,"
Rachel's mother objects,
"but being a full-time painter
is for ladies with rich husbands.
That's not Ken, at least not lately.
So now I'm aiming for a marketable career."
"Dr. Freud, move over,"
snaps Rachel, and she winks at me.
"Dr. Freud would love me," challenges Kiki,
not even a little bit annoyed.
"He'd appreciate me,
unlike some people I know . . ."
She tosses a sly look at Rachel.
Then she grins.
"You must think we're nutty, Maisie!"
That's the last thing I think.

NO SENSE TO ME

Somehow, I'm speaking quickly,
my words tumbling over one another.
I'm telling them both that I love to draw.
That in my family, art

is about handmade cocktail dresses
and needlepoint pillows.
Which somehow gets me going about Judith.
Then I'm saying that my mother's a complete bitch,
that my brother is more secretive than the FBI,
that my father keeps taking mysterious business trips
and travels on jet planes with movie stars
and refers to Mayor Wagner
by his first name, Robert!
That our house always reeks
of the most recent perfume he's developing.
That he's planning to leave us.

Sentences stream out of me,
maybe because Rache and Kiki seem to want to hear
what I have to say.
"In my master's program," says Kiki,
"I'm learning that all families have warts and dings,
slings and arrows. People are taught they have to hide the truth."
"My family's practically a combat unit,"
I blurt.
Kiki mumbles that sometimes trouble
can become alchemized
so that it turns into something valuable.
I think trouble is trouble, isn't it?
Kiki pauses, says, "Combat unit? Explain."
"The other night my mother told me
I belong in a mental hospital!
I said right to her face,
'After you, Mom.
You're turning me into a horrible person.
And I don't want to be a horrible person.'"

GLUB, GLUB

Rachel's and her mom's faces go blank.
"I'm sorry. I'm talking too much.
I sound like a pathetic loser."
Kiki says, "It's okay!
It's good to get stuff off your chest."
She turns to Rachel and says,
"This is a good one."
How could such a mess of a girl
be a "good one"?
What if they knew;
if they only knew that most days
I only feel like one quarter of a human being,
three quarters longing,
drowning in emptiness,
like one of those Magritte paintings
where you see clouds
right through the middle of the person.
If they knew that my heart is broken,
that I wish I could stick a pin in my head
like a homemade lobotomy,
to make certain feelings disappear,
that a part of myself is underwater,
glub, glub,
that I wish I was a member of another species,
a dolphin, maybe,
so I could swim or play a little.
Or an orangutan (they seem to enjoy themselves).
Rachel and her mom would change their minds about me,
and I'd be finished in their cool, artsy house
with the glass rainbows
and the dark-blue wall
forever.

DINNER

Jake and Jonathan, Rachel and I
set the table for dinner
like it's the most natural thing in the world.
Rachel whispers, "Sleepover?
My parents will forget to bother me if you're around.
Please?"
Kiki brings in a huge platter.
"Greeks make the best lamb,"
says Rachel proudly.
Kiki and Ken toast each other
with a glass of Mavrodaphne.
"I wish my parents would drink wine,"
I say. "But they're dead set against relaxing."
"A glass, maybe," mutters Rachel,
"but not an entire bottle!
Do you see them?
Lushes! That's why I don't drink.
I never will."

THE DAMN ROAST

"At least your parents
don't hide anything, Rachel."
I watch them tease each other
in a friendly way, as if it's a game,
not a blood sport.
Ken's complaining about the roast.
"Overdone!"
Kiki's saying, "Next time you can cook it yourself."
Ken says fine, after work he'll drive up
the Cross Bronx Expressway.
So what if he left home at 7 A.M.?
He'll put on an apron
and shove the damn thing into the oven.
Kiki toasts him, says "I *love* that idea!"
"It will be ready at nine, the earliest,"
he continues.
"You forgot, Ken—I'm a night bird.
Then we can go downtown
and listen to some jazz
at the Village Vanguard."

ON THE CHEEK

Ken's laughing, says,
"Can't win with your mother, kids!"
Then he says, "I love this dish!
Anyway, who needs seasoning?
Not me! No sirree!"
He gets up, walks around the table,
and kisses Kiki on the cheek
as if they were in a Doris Day movie.
Rachel rolls her eyes.
"They do this to embarrass me, Maisie.
It really gets old."
It's not old to me.
To me, it's brand-new
to watch parents argue then kiss and hug
right in front of their kids.
You can tell they're crazy about each other.

FILL IN THE BLANKS

After dinner Rachel stacks plates,
the brothers wash them,
and then I dry and help put away the dishes.
Kiki puts the leftovers away,
tells me about her days as an art student.
When the kitchen is humming
and clean, she brings out some notebooks
and we talk a little about anatomy.
She gives me a newsprint sketch pad and some charcoal
to keep at their house.
She says drawing just about saved her life.
I want to ask her from what?

But I don't dare.
I feel as if I've always known her.
When we're falling asleep, I finally decide
to pester Rache about this boy—Gino.
But by the time I do,
there's light snoring.

IDIOT

Mindlessly riding on the good feelings from Rachel's,
I walk home in the bright Saturday morning
without suppressing a rare feeling
of naked enthusiasm for simply being alive.
The clouds overhead filter out
the sun and diffuse the light,
which makes everything appear a little gauzy,
painterly, and sublimely benevolent.
But I'm an idiot.
Because bouncing home,
especially bouncing home *joyfully*,
is a stupid act.
I should know by now there will be hell to pay.

I pass our mailbox.
There's a note on pink paper from Richie.
I grab it and thrust it into my jacket.
Richie, I ask him silently, what are you doing?

OUTLAW JOY

I run into the house, forgetting to hide
this dumb, outlawed exuberance.
"You had a good time?"
Judith is spraying her red hair into a helmet.
"They were so nice," I say.
Immediately I regret it, tamp down my voice.
"I mean, it was kind of okay."
But Judith has already gotten the message
that I prefer them to her.
She stops with her hair.
She's already dipping down
into that dark mood again.
"Wipe that dumb look off your face!
I'm mad at you, you moronic girl!"
Like a once-damp towel, dried in the sun,
my restraint evaporates from the warmth of
Rachel's loving tribe.
And I spit out my truth:
"Of course you're mad.
You're always mad.
At everyone all the time!"

I can only imagine
the consequences of my outburst.

PRISONERS

The next day Davy and I are on the escalator
in Macy's department store.
Mother's prisoners.
I point out the boys' section to Davy.
"Don't you want some new clothes?"
"Davy, do *not* let your sister goad you
into being a nuisance.
One in the family is enough," says Judith.
But it *is* my job to goad Davy.
One in the family is *not* enough.
Because if you're that one, you're in for it.

"I need new cords . . . ," says Davy.
Mother mumbles:
"Davy, Maisie's only trouble.
Don't copy her!"
She says my name
as if it leaves a bad taste in her mouth.
"Davy." I nudge him.
"Tell her I'm not that bad."
Davy ignores me.
I figure one day, inevitably,
the tables will turn.
We'll see what happens then.

THE SHOE DEPARTMENT OF LIFE

We're shopping because
clothes are Judith's passion.
And shoes. She loves shoes.
She doesn't like salesmen.
Anyway, generally she prefers
inanimate objects to people.

I've seen Buddy, Harvey, and Benny,
who've worked at Macy's forever,
flee to the back room when they spot her.
I bet they toss a coin.
Nobody would choose to deal with her
when she's in one of her moods.
And she always is.

SKINNY KID

This afternoon, Benny turns to Ernest,
the new guy, neat, slim,
skin the color of hot chocolate.
He's maybe a college kid.
"It's your turn, E," Benny says.
Ernest walks up to us with a nervous smile,
glances at me, says in a low, silky, musical voice,
"Hello, what can I get you?"
My mother thrusts out a pointy, high-heeled number
she took from the display.
"In nine and nine and a half, also ten.
I don't trust your sizes," she adds,
as if Ernest personally manufactures the shoes
to confound her.

He turns to Davy:
"And hello to you, too, young man.
How's your day going?"
"Bring it in navy, brown, beige,"
she says in her most pebbly, aggravating voice.
"And for you, little lady?" He winks at me.
With worried eyes, I sing out, "I'm Maisie."
"Anything for you, Maisie?"
"Mom?" I say, eyebrows high.
Judith clucks. "She doesn't need a thing."
But, Ernest, I think, I need lots of things.

THE EXISTENTIAL OBSERVATION

I like his wide, toothy, white smile.
Zombielike, I follow him to the rear of the store.
Through the heavy curtains guarding the stockroom,
I hear the guys in the back room titter.
"Thanks for the help, boys," Ernest jokes.
With a plastered smile, he reemerges,
balances the piled-up boxes,
which he lays in front of Judith.

Her feet are long and skinny.
When you don't like someone,
it's funny how you don't like their feet, either.
This is my existential observation.

LIKE A GANGSTER

"Get me an insert!" My mother's nasal voice
is an accusation.
"Of course!" Ernest replies, as if her request
has made him happy!
He flees toward the back room.
I trail him again.
The guys are making bets as to how long
it'll take for my mother to go completely bonkers.
Ernest sighs, winks as he passes me
on the way back to her.
She slips the pad in.
"The insole is wrong for me!"
She orders another style.
He finally says, "I don't think
you're going to like
how that one will feel, either.
The last is cut wide."
"Who the hell asked you?"
She barks like a gangster.
He stiffens a bit, returns to the storeroom,
balancing all the boxes.
My mother smiles.
She loves shopping for shoes,
but she hates spending money.

FIND THE MANAGER!

She rifles through everything.
"I don't like these! Find the manager!"
She gives me a look that would go well with a gun.
Ernest uses a soothing voice
that probably works with children.
"The manager can only tell you
what I already explained: I'm real sorry,
but we don't have this style in narrow.
Why don't I bring out a shoe
that would be beautiful *and* comfortable for you?"
Ernest gives her a strained grin,
which shows off those perfect teeth.

WHAT'S SO FUNNY?

Another salesman appears.
"Is Ernest giving you any problems,
madam?" he asks gravely.
"He's trying to help," I offer.
"He's not helping *me*," Judith pouts.
"I'm so sorry," he says, all soft and solicitous.
What is this guy up to?
"You know what, lady?"
He kneels down.
"Call me Judith," she corrects.
"Miss Judith, you know what?
I have just the solution.
I'm going to fire Ernest's skinny black ass."
My mother's voice rises.
"This has nothing to do with the color of his skin!"

Judith is a lot of things.
But
she's no racist.
Now, from the back room,
another guy appears and cracks up.
"What's so funny?" Judith barks.
"Maybe you could lighten up, lady,"
says Benny.
"Where I come from, people would be thrilled
to be busting their brains over which pair
of seventy-five-dollar shoes to buy
and put on their smelly, dog-ugly feet."

IRONIC

My mother bolts up,
slides into her pumps,
heads for the door.
In the back, the guys slap one another's backs.
I hear one of them say,
"Heck, from now on,
we should all just share commissions!"
I think how ironic it is that my nasty mother
and her bad attitude
brought the sales team together.

MAP OF THE WORLD

As Judith stomps toward the escalator,
I spot Richie!
He's in the boys' section,
studying a sweater
as if it were a map of the world.

"Don't you want to look at the scarves, Mom?"
I ask, trying to direct her away from Richie.
"Scarves are fifties, not sixties, right, Davy?!"
she says disdainfully,
as if, somehow, my brother is her fashion consultant.
She points at Richie.
"Isn't that your friend?"
she asks, but the word *friend* sounds like *ax murderer*
on her lips.
"Oh! Yes! But he's shy, Mom.
I can see him later."
I will her to keep walking.
"Richie!" she commands.
Behind her, I wave meekly,
trying to transmit "run, Richie, *run*,"
but he walks over, unsuspecting.
Who I see is a smart guy
who speaks French,
quotes James Joyce,
is trying to survive his father's wrath;
who has plans for his future
and lifts boxes
in the freezing back rooms of the Safeway.
Who likes me.
My mother sees a skinny kid
wearing threadbare clothes.
A shabby haircut and a hesitant, self-effacing manner.
"Hi, Mrs. Meyers,"
Richie says, holding a hanger
with a navy vest.
"Let me see what you're buying, son,"
she says in her most beguiling voice.
Uh-oh.

MAPLE SYRUP

I wish I could warn him: *This is a trap!*
As he hands the vest over,
I wait for her to come in for the kill.
"You have good taste." She smiles.
"I need your opinion, young man.
You and Maisie are tight.
So is she a royal pain in the ass
to you, too?"
Richie sort of hops backward as if he were pushed.
I see his eyebrows coming together in effort.
His chin juts forward just a bit.
Guileless, he looks directly at my mother.
"If I had to characterize Maisie"—
he winks at me—
"I'd say she's more of a rebel.
That is one of the things I like best
about her, Mrs. Meyers."
"Then you're an idiot, Richie."
"Mother!" I sputter. "*Stop* it!"
She laughs. Well, cackles.
I hiss and roll my eyes.
She catches me in the act.
"Don't you dare give me that face!"
Her arm springs out and shoves me back
into a clothes rack.
I frantically grab on to something, a jacket,
thus bringing a bundle of new clothes down
with me as I tumble to the floor.
"Look at your idiot sister, Davy!"
Judith grabs my brother

and drags him toward the elevator.
She throws Richie the navy vest.
"Ugly! Go home, kid!"

"Maisie, Maisie . . . ," Richie calls;
his maple syrup voice floods me
with hope.

EXCEPT IF YOU'RE A CAT

When I get home,
I call Rachel and refashion my story.
The version I tell her has me on the floor,
covered in designer labels, the only way
I'll ever get close to Emilio Pucci, ha ha . . .
my mother tapping her foot in her old, *not* new pumps . . .
Rachel jumps in: "I get it.
My entire family is crazy, too,
except I'm not sure about the dog.
Well, come to think of it, the dog is nutty also,
mostly in an interesting way.
Except if you're a cat."

CATCH-22

When Rachel thinks I'm upset,
or when she's upset, or sometimes
when neither one of us is upset,
she likes to quote *Catch-22*.
Test right before Thanksgiving.
Firm deadline.

"I adore Heller," she says.
She recalls the part where Yossarian
does the kindness of pretending to be
the dying son of a family
so his parents can say
their final goodbye to him.
"It's a killer scene, Maisie!" she says.
"The father says to Yossarian,
who's pretending to be dead Guiseppe,
that when he gets to see God,
'You'll be just as good as anybody else
in heaven, even though you *are Italian*.'
It's so non sequitur!" she squeals.
"How about this one?" I match her.
"'He felt awkward
because she was going to murder him.'"
Heller cracks us up.

In a tremulous voice I barely recognize,
she says randomly,
"Maisie, this boy, Gino . . ."
"Yes?"
"Can't say any more yet." She giggles.
Rachel's a hearty laugher, a knee-slapper,
a real guffawer.
She's not a delicate girly giggler.
It's a warning!
I don't want a boy coming between us
is what I think.

FREAK FOR GERSHWIN

The next morning I listen
as Davy practices Gershwin
on the mahogany upright.
The piano is the only piece of furniture
not wrapped in plastic.
When you sit on our couch it squeaks!
My mother loves order.
"I bet you wish you could wrap us in plastic, too,"
I have muttered sotto voce more than once.

Sometimes, when I wish Davy
and I were closer,
I ask him about Tin Pan Alley;
Gershwin is his favorite subject.
"George was always in trouble.
like *you*, Maisie," he says,
"except *he* was a total genius.
He skipped school on the Lower East Side,
loved to roller skate
and listen to the sounds of the streets.
He was lucky to have a brother, Ira.
I wish I had a brother."
If that's a dig, I decide not to play.
"Did you know he was Jewish?!"
I ask, then show him my list of famous Jews.
"Why do you care?" he asks.
"Grandma thinks it's important to remind ourselves
that the Nazis didn't get us," I say.
"And they never will.
She says the war only ended sixteen years ago.
And we can't forget it,

no matter how difficult
it is to remember."
His beautiful eyes take that in.
I give him a light love tap.

IT'S A START

Finally he says, "Oh!"
"Oh." It's a start, I guess.
When Davy talks to me,
it opens a window between us,
and there comes a gentle breeze
that touches us both.

SAFETY ZONE

The trick to keeping the house from exploding
is for Joe to continue
to come home for dinner.
That means Every. Single. Night.
At least for a while.
It's been three days so far.
Fingers crossed.
Before we eat my mother comes into my room
and helps me put my clothes away
without scolding me once.
She picks up one of my drawings,
actually says, "Interesting!"
then winks at me
as if suddenly we are buddies.
How long can that last?
There've been some sonic rumblings,
but so far there's no actual storm.

The mood in our apartment
tends to build like a weather front.
Tonight after dinner,
I begin to feel the tension again.
The beige walls become oppressive.
Instead of doing my algebra equations,
I find myself fluffing my pillows
trying to cheer the room up
as if it were in a bad mood.

A DIFFERENT LIFE

Washing the dishes,
my mother starts complaining,
dressing my father down.
Why does she do that?
She should speak more softly to him.
Maybe smile once in a while.
In any case, her tone sends him
to our fire escape.
He lights up.
I look out the window,
imagine that sitting out there, alone,
watching the smoke curl and disappear,
gives my dad some peace of mind.
I wonder if, when he looks up at the moon,
he wishes for a different life,
far away from Parkchester
and East Tremont Avenue,
far away from a home
where everyone's on edge and, any minute,
like gasoline mixing with oxygen,
my mother might combust
right in front of us.

OUTSIDE

I wrap myself in a wool sweater
Grandma Ruth made for me—
Hungarians are prodigious knitters—
and I slide open the heavy glass door.
I'm his favorite. He even says that.
More than once—when Davy isn't around, of course.
I wipe the dusty chairs,
move my mother's rosebush,
sit myself down next to him.

THE CITY

The tiny fire escape is our private spot.
He says he's sorry he's gone so often.
Do I remember when I was six
and he took me into Manhattan?
I wore a red coat, red shoes,
and perfect white leather gloves
embroidered with tiny blue buds.
I recall watching the road into the city:
billboards, telephone lines, bridges,
muddy sky.
The parking garage man said,
"So you're the boss man's little lady
I've heard so much about?"
The elevator man, Jimmy,
knew my name!
My dad's corner office had the most windows,
the biggest desk, too.
My father bragged, "Your daddy runs this joint!"
From his window, as it got dark,

we could see Manhattan laid out in front of us
like a glittering tablecloth.

How could I not remember?
It was a perfect day,
until he turned the key in our front door.
Mother was waiting.

DIRTY HABIT

A breeze pushes the fumes against my face.
He snuffs out a butt, then lights another,
says, "Look, kid, smoking's a dirty habit.
I'm going to quit soon."
"That's what Miss Volk,
my homeroom teacher, says," I offer.
"Who?" he asks.
"Miss Volk, the one you thought
was pretty."
He never remembers anything I tell him.
"Oh!" he says, and now he's smiling.
He has a photographic memory
when he finds anyone appealing.

"Teach me to smoke!" I say.
His eyebrows meet above his nose,
and as the tip of the cigarette burns,
it sends smoke into the clear night
like a signal.
Maybe, across the Harlem River
someone will see it,
realize we are signaling: Help!

THE FUTURE

"Let me try it, please? I want to be like you!"
"No, you don't! Not now, not ever."
"But, Dad, at least I should know
what I'll be missing for the rest of my life."
He smiles so wide, I can see his molars.
"Well, you never know about the future,"
he says, ominously.
I grab his arm.
"Tell me the truth.
Are you thinking of leaving?"
"Leaving what?"
"Dad!"
"What?"
"*Us!* Please! Please don't leave!
You can't. I mean it!
She hates me."
"Calm down, Maisie," he says.
My voice crackles.
"I'm just telling you, if you go,
she'll put me in the ground."
He ruffles my hair
as if I am being amusing.
I want to scream.

DADDY, DADDY, DADDY

I was five the first time he left.
It would've been different then,
because his dying would have been
against his will;
he wouldn't have been a *leaver*.

That morning I'd watched the clouds
shed faucets of rain, chanting,
"Daddy, Daddy, Daddy."
I couldn't wait for him to come home
and save me.
Finally, a telephone call from Chicago!
I could hear Daddy's special, Maisie-only voice:
"Are you drawing me some pictures?
I need a new one for my office.
I'll be home tonight!"

NEVER

After dinner, almost bedtime,
Grandma galloped through the door,
turned on the TV.
The newscaster said a lot of words
I didn't understand,
but I did hear one: *airplane.*
Screaming.
Judith and Grandma were both screaming so loud!
"There was a plane crash,"
said the man on TV.
Daddy was never coming home.
Not soon. Not later. *Never.*
Then *I* was screaming.
Grandma caught me, tried to rock me.
He couldn't be gone.
If I ever saw him again, I'd punch him so hard.

FLOWERED DRESS

Grandma gave me a glass of something
that smelled like it came from the dry cleaner.
I sipped it, but it burned my tongue.
I spit it out.
Then I threw up, ran the hot water,
put my hands under the faucet until they burned.
Outside, the sky was getting light
like it was another regular day.
I cuddled next to Grandma,
pushing into her flowered dress
as if by climbing inside it,
I'd turn into a daisy
and stop being a little girl.

DEAD DADDY

The sun began to rise.
I stayed in bed.
This day could not happen.
I heard the front door bang wide open.
A voice . . . an excited voice, rang out.
It belonged to dead daddy!
He charged in, threw his hat down.
I leaped out of bed and lunged at him,
buried my head between his knees,
which I gripped powerfully.
He bent down and whispered,
"It's okay, monkey.
I took a later flight."
I gripped him even tighter.
My mother pushed me aside.

I thought she wanted to hug him.
But she didn't. She yelled.
"Bastard! You couldn't have called?
What you put me through!"
His eyes found mine.
Even I knew they were heartbroken.
That was the day I realized
he knew how she got.

ONE PUFF

"Do you think I'm a rotten kid?"
"You're a great kid, Maisie."
"I'm trying to reform, Dad."
"Maisie, honey,
I like you exactly the way you are:
spirited, smart, your own person."
"Being my own person
is treacherous," I say.
He turns to me.
"Are you working me over?" he asks.
I know not to answer.
"Okay, you poor kid, one puff.
I'll give you *one* shot at it,
but you have to do exactly what I say.
You have to learn how to inhale, okay?"

I do have to learn how to inhale.
How to breathe,
as if I belong here on the earth.

SO ALIKE

I look at his face,
think how I'm glad he breaks the rules.
He says we're alike.
That must be why I'm the way I am,
as my grandma likes to say,
always flirting with disaster,
as if disaster was my middle name.

UNDERWATER

"When you smoke,
you take in the deepest breath,
as if you have to last underwater
without air.
Then you keep it in
as long as you possibly can."
"But you don't do that, Dad."
"I've been smoking a long time, kid.
Ready?" he says, and lights a fresh one.
I sit up tall under the stars,
put my feet on the step,
straighten my back
so I can always remember
this moment, me and my dad,
on the same wavelength.
Me, trying to figure out
if he wants to protect me
while he's teaching me to smoke.

HOLD IT IN

A door slams.
I jump.
From across the courtyard
comes a jumble of curses
even though all the windows are closed
against the cool winter afternoon.
It's Richie's parents again.
My dad and I stop talking.
"Richie's father is so angry,"
I say. "Mom and Mr. O'Neill
could have a nightclub act.
'Tonight we present,
from the dismal heart of the Bronx,
Judith and Brian, the Anger Twins.
Order a drink and watch them fume!'"
"Maisie, honey,
I don't think this should be your worry.
How about filling me in on your classes?"
He sighs, offers the cigarette.
"School has its moments," I say,
and close my lips around the tobacco,
inhale really, really deeply.
I am about to show him the bruises
I still have on my arm,
but then the smoke curls in my chest,
which immediately wants to explode.
"Hold it in," he commands.
"Don't let it out."
Finally my mouth opens
because I'm coughing and gasping.
It feels like some kind of torture.

The taste is nasty.
"It's awful!" I cough.
"It tastes horrible, feels horrible."
I'm practically crying.
"So disgusting! How could you?!"
My dad laughs.
"Well, now you never have to become a smoker!"

THE LEAVING DEPARTMENT

I dash inside, refuse to speak to him
for the rest of the night.
"I'm done with you, Dad!"
He laughs!
Later he knocks on my door,
takes my hand.
"Between you and me,
if anything ever happened—
not that it will—in the leaving department,
wherever I'd go,
you'd be coming with me, kid.
I promise."
I throw my arms around him.
Later I will drift off wondering
how much warning he'd give me.
And what about my brother?

SECRETS

I go into Davy's room, sit on his bed, announce,
"I'm never going to smoke."
He looks at me blankly.
"What about you, Davy?"
"I hate school," he says. "I don't fit in."
"Can't you find someone else
who likes Gershwin?" I ask.
"You don't understand *anything*,"
he says, and turns off his light.
I wish Davy could be like the rascal kid brother
you see on every other TV sitcom.
But there are no sitcoms
that anyone in this family could be in.

WHO I WANT TO TALK ABOUT

In the morning, my father knocks on my door,
sipping from his coffee mug.
"You almost killed me by cigarette,"
I shout. "I decided I'm still mad at you!"
He walks in anyway, smiling.
Naturally.
He's always been overconfident.
"I did not almost kill you, kid."
He sits at my desk chair
and swivels around toward me,
his big gray-green eyes wide open, earnest.
"I want to talk to you about your brother.
I'm trying to understand him.
Don't you want to help?"
My dad puts his feet up on my bed

and gets comfortable.
"I'm not speaking to you!"
I sulk. Davy's not who I want to talk about.

PRAY HARDER

But I know what he's getting at.
I was there yesterday
when Davy told my dad
that the yellow-tinted sweater he was wearing
was not a good color for him.
"Your skin looks sallow," said Davy.
"You should try more of a butterscotch."
"Butterscotch?" My dad's face went white,
as if he'd heard a swear word.
"Is that actually a color?"
he asked incredulously.
Now, sipping his coffee, he says:
"Maisie, from a son, I expect dirty underwear,
curse words, fart jokes.
But what kind of boy cares about *colors*?"
"I like colors. Maybe it runs in the family."
He sighs, gets up, turns, and says:
"Life is hard if you're different.
Hell, it's hard enough if you're not!"
"I already know that!" I grumble.
"I pray Davy grows out of it, Maisie,
but maybe I need to pray harder."
"I think you should worry about *me*, Dad."
My father pauses.
Then he turns back and stares into my eyes
as if trying to memorize my face.

LUNCH BREAK

Outside, at lunch break, I watch kids
lighting up, thinking they're so cool.
Richie's dusty-blue eyes stare at a cigarette
as if it holds some secret information.
Now I know these smokers are unlucky.
They don't have a father
who makes them inhale, cough, choke,
and almost puke
and get a headache
and be miserable for hours.
They haven't been taught a lesson.
My lungs will last a lifetime.
On the other hand, maybe their dads
didn't teach them not to smoke
because they weren't planning on going anywhere.

A FUNERAL DOES

A piece of pink paper falls out of my pocket.
It's the note Richie gave me
that I stuck away days ago.
Rather upsets a man's day,
a funeral does.
—James Joyce
That's the *only* thing he wrote!
Damn! Richie's freaking me out.

I don't see him all day, so
after school I cross over to his building,
ride up to the sixth floor, and knock.
Frizzy-haired Regina answers.
"He's at work already," she says,

shutting the door in my face
before I can even say thanks.
Clearly she's like her brother, another member
of the Introverts R Us gang.

SAFEWAY

I trudge over to Safeway,
locate Richie in the back, sweeping.
He smiles when he sees me,
but then, he probably guesses why I'm here,
decides to educate me.
He saunters over to the produce.
"You never want to buy lettuce
that has any brown leaves,"
he says.
"And you want to see what's on special.
Carrots get moldy.
You have to really pay attention
in case they're old.
Always touch red peppers;
they should be hard, not soft."
"Stop! Just stop, Professor Greengrocer!
Why are you writing sad,
scary notes about funerals,
and why to *me*, Richie?"
"You finally read that?
It's James Joyce!" he says,
heading back into the storage room.
"I thought it was a funny line."
I'm following him. "Funny?"
"Or at least droll?"
"Nothing about death is funny, Richie!

Or droll.
And certainly not one line, out of context.
Now if you want to slip on a banana peel,
that would be funny."
"Really? You sure?"
"I'm sure."
So then he does.
He takes a banana, peels it,
throws the skin down, runs up to it,
and does a pratfall.
From the floor,
he looks up at me hopefully.
"You're crazy, Richie O'Neill!" I laugh.
He smiles wide, so satisfied.
"Okay, you got me!"

POOF!

He gets up with sawdust on his pants.
"Here's how I see it," he says.
"We're here on planet Earth,
worried about mundane,
meaningless stuff all the time,
like your French teacher picks on you,
and your dad's going a little nuts,
then, poof, you're gone forever.
Sure, then other people are upset,
but you're fine."
"How can you be fine if you're dead?
And *why* are you so morbid?"
"I'm not morbid!"
"Well, I worry you're trying to tell me something
about your disastrous state of mind!

Maybe you should see the guidance counselor?"
Richie picks up a red cabbage
and sticks it in front of the other ones.
"Number one, I just made you laugh.
More importantly, I'm a poet.
Poets don't talk to guidance counselors!"

IT'S JAMES JOYCE!

"Well, if you're going to keep writing notes to me,
write something that is amusing,
not things I can't understand."
He looks surprised.
"Hey, sorry, Maisie.
But you should read James Joyce!"
"I should," I say. "I will.
And then I'll write you some terse,
Irish-y hair-raising sentences!"
"You really don't need to get in a twist."
"I'm not in a twist!"
"I think you *are* in a twist," he says.
"Should I fall down again?
Is that your cultural reference point?"
Then, before I know what I'm saying,
I blurt: "You know what?
This conversation is over!"
"Excellent!" he says. "Now what?"

"I'll tell you what."
And right in the cold storage room
I lean into him.
"Kiss me!" I command.
"Huh?"

"It's my birthday soon.
I need something to happen!"
"I forgot it's your birthday,"
he says thoughtfully.
"Stop stalling, Richie!"
So he steps closer and puts his lips on my cheek.
"Not *that* kind of a kiss!" I almost holler.
"Which kind do you want, Maisie?"
I turn and leave, fed up.
"Wait!" he calls after me.
"I mean, I need to be more prepared!"
"It's not a quiz on verb conjugation!"
I shout back.
He hollers something, but I feel like a fool
and outrun his silly voice.

SOCKS

I soothe myself by folding my dad's socks.
These days, my mom just throws them
in his drawer unmatched, helter-skelter.
I have to stay on his good side.
At least he has a good side.
Browns, grays, navies, and a few
let's-get-down-to-business-and-make-a-deal blacks.
A muddy cotton palette.
"What are you doing in here?"
Judith stomps into the hallway
where the bureau is,
as if I'm doing something underhanded.
"He says he can never find matching socks," I say.
"Well, he doesn't deserve matching socks!"
She throws the new cotton couplets

I made on the carpet as if to punish them,
I guess for covering his feet.
"I know what you're up to, Maisie!"
"WHAT I'M UP TO is being a kid
who likes her dad!"

I SEE THUNDER

"Stupid, stupid girl, he doesn't care about you!"
I can't help myself. I say,
"I wouldn't be surprised
if one day my father skedaddles out of here.
I'll be leaving with him."
The blows come.
On my arms, my back, my face.
I tremble, fold up my spine
to protect against her wild hands,
I'm growing a hard kernel of meanness inside.
I'm getting stony, cold and stubborn.
I will not let her murder me
like it's her job,
a little, day by day.
She's ice. I'm fire.
When I look in the mirror, I see thunder.
At our house it's always war.

A MILLION QUESTIONS

Tonight, my dad arrives before dinner.
He throws open the front door
as if he's the star of a cabaret act,
grabs the Ping-Pong racket, sings out:
"Who wants to play me?"
Neither Davy nor I say a word.
But he starts tapping the ball invitingly,
so I grab a racket.
"It's January. I was born in January,"
I remind him.
"Happy birthday, kiddo," he says, and serves.
I can tell he's thinking about other things.
"You remember my secretary, Shirley,
curly dark-brown hair and nice-looking?"
Why does he think I'd want to hear
about who he finds attractive?
"This morning she comes in, says:
'You don't look happy, Mr. M.'"
My dad talks about women
like some guys talk about sports cars.
He's obsessed.
Then he winks, as if I'm a member
of the potential cheaters club.
I slam the ball, win the point,
then I walk away, fuming.
Ping-Pong brings out the worst in him.
And me.

WALLPAPER

He throws his racket down, too.
Then, out of the blue,
points to our sole green wall,
says, "Green! I just hate that color,"
loud enough for my mother to hear.
I say, "I know what you mean."
But I don't.
Then I remember the swatches
in the back seat of my mother's car.
A few weeks ago, she'd picked one up
and said, almost gaily,
"What do you think, Maisie?
It's for the living room.
It's rich, isn't it?"
"What's it called, Mom?"
"What does it matter?"
"I'm not sure," I said.
"You say you're an artist.
Can't you see it's rich?
It'll go with the new wallpaper."
"But we don't have wallpaper
in the living room, Mom."
"We will soon."
I don't know what's going on with them.
But I wish I could hold up a traffic sign.
DETOUR. Or EXIT AHEAD. Or STOP!

OLIVE

In the morning, three painters
are scraping our walls.
They work until 5 P.M., return for two more days,
then paste green paisley wallpaper
in the dining room,
dark-green paisley
in the living room.
The next night, when my dad makes it home,
he throws down his cashmere overcoat
and whips around to my mother:
"What the hell? What did you do?"
"Calm down, Joe," she says.
Davy retreats to his room.
He hates fighting,
hates it on TV, hates it in school.
Soon he'll be banging his head,
blotting us all out.
I hate fighting, too.
I wonder, how badly can they fight about a *color*?
"I told you, no green!"
my father roars.
"It's not green, Joe, it's olive!"
"Olive *is* green!" He stomps around.
"The color, Judith, is called olive *green*."
She must know that to my father,
green means the army,
fatigues, bombs, bullets, chaos.
So many boys he was drafted with
were maimed, destroyed, dead.
And there's our people,
who had our blood, our eyes—

who didn't get out of Europe in time
and were decimated.
So I guess this too-green house
is her announcement
of a new siege.

SOONER NOT LATER

One of my dad's perfumes has taken off.
He says he's rich now.
All weekend, he plays golf
at his new country club in Riverdale.
He says I can have a sweet sixteen there.
Then he kids me about getting older.
He loves to tease me.
"Wow, you're practically ancient."
He forgets how old I am. I'm turning fifteen.
But he's distracted, I guess.
Then on Monday morning
he drives down to Manhattan
with his overnight bag.
The painters return that afternoon,
finish the remaining walls
in a deep forest green.
Drop cloths everywhere, furniture mummies crowding together.
I don't have the courage to say,
"Mom, what are you thinking?
Dad hates green."
But my grandmother does.
"Daughter, vhy do you have to make Joe feel
that vhen he comes home, he's on parole?"
Right in front of us,
my mother yells at her mother.

My grandma grabs her coat
and, without saying a word,
packs up her homemade stuffed cabbage
and leaves!
Judith sends out for soggy Chinese.

I PROMISE MYSELF

It's Saturday.
Maybe because of our stupid ugly walls,
my father has totally, completely
forgotten my age and my birthday!
Not a word. Not a card.
It looks as if he's truly gone.
I'm fifteen. Finally, fifteen.
I close the curtains so Richie
can't spy on me looking at myself.
My body's starting to explode.
The hair is thickening between my legs.
My skin is smooth, creamy.
My nipples a pleasing peachy brown.
I touch the curve of my fine ass.
I want to be adored.
I want to shout to the world:
"I'm inside here!"
I want to scream, "Look into my eyes.
Lick me. Touch me!
Somebody ravish me!"
I glance through my curtains toward Richie's.
"Not you, Richie. You blew it!"
But then, before I can think another thought,
I part the curtains anyway!
What am I doing?

But he is a boy, after all.
If he'd look at me, then I'd know
what that feels like.
I'd know if there's any lust in his heart
with my name on it.
Then I wonder, am I an upcoming slut
or only a hormone-hot teenager?
Or is this just what happens
when your body realizes
it can make babies?

NEVER MIND

My mother's taking Davy to his music lesson.
It's like they're the ones
who are married in this family.
Bugs in a rug.
Not a word about this being my birthday
from either one of them.
It's cold out, mean cold.
Tomorrow I'll stop by my grandma's,
but today I'm going to Rachel's.
Last time I was there, I asked Kiki,
"For my birthday, could I visit your studio?"
Rachel jumped in, said,
"Wow! I mean, sure,
I wanted a sister
and I love you madly, Maisie,
but not every minute of every day!"
Kiki gave Rache a severe look, said,
"Since when are you a brat, Rache?!
I don't raise bratty kids!"
"Sorry. I'd just planned to be there to draw Gino!"

Rachel said. "Alone!"
"Never mind," I said quickly.
"Forget it! Bad idea."
"It's a good idea.
Just don't fall for my boyfriend, Maisie.
Promise?"
"Promise."
"Okay! It's a plan.
I want my best friend
to have a good birthday."
"Of course you do," said Kiki.
So I hugged them both.

TIME IS A DUST CLOUD

This day, the day I was born, I'm alone.
Time hangs like a dust cloud.
The sky is overcast.
It's as if yesterday's sunshine never happened.
Looking out the window again,
I see Judith's Buick shoot down the street,
an infuriated bullet.
Today, once again, I promise myself
that I won't, as if in a trance,
sneak into her bedroom, to her closet.
It's a ritual I do every single week.
I have to stop.
I open up my algebra textbook.
But equations are so neat.
There's no algebra
that can explain my messy life.
I decide to wash a few dirty dishes.
They can be wiped clean,

but how do you get a haunted girl,
full of mute hungers, to sparkle?
Maybe, though, I can just peek into my mother's closet
and then quit my covert forays forever
and even leave this cell block of a house.
That's a plan!

LEAVING EARTH

I turn on the radio for company.
According to a news report,
this very day, January 17, 1961,
will be remembered in history!
Yuri Gagarin, the Russian cosmonaut,
has been selected to pilot a Soviet spacecraft.
It will be thrust into orbit at 18,000 miles per hour.
He grew up in a mud hut
and soon he'll be in a capsule,
completely alone, where nobody has ever been,
the first human to orbit Earth.
I love him for this with all my heart.
I try to imagine what he will see.
What does space look like?
How will he like being weightless?
I feel as if I'm carrying around
so much more than my own 114 pounds.

COMPULSION

Once again I find myself
entering my mother's wardrobe.
Conquering outer space
is no longer of interest to me.
Judith's clothes—dresses, jackets, pants, skirts—
a cloth core of well-behaved operatives,
are clustered together, ready to serve her
at a moment's notice.
The fabrics are smooth, luxurious,
silks, merino wool, cashmere.
I begin tirelessly working zippers,
buttons, rearranging collars, belts,
like a mindless robot.
I'm trained in my mission
as much as Gagarin will train for his.
I have no thoughts except how I can get through
the entire collection before she returns.
It's a terrible, dumb compulsion.
And it's nerve-racking, that's for sure.

STEALING

Today she took off suddenly.
For a moment I thought, of course,
she'll be getting a cake for me.
Then I realized that random thought
might apply to mothers in general.
But with mine, it's not remotely possible.
That's not what she's up to.
Bye, Ma.
She won't celebrate me.
She'll never lend me anything, either.
So I'm stealing.
But I tell myself you really can't steal
from your own mother, can you?
Especially if, when you shut the closet,
nothing's missing.

I wonder why she's never noticed that
her clothes are rearranged, out of order,
unlike the perfectly ordered garments
she left a few hours ago.
I'm up to the skirts, fitted numbers
that hang loose on me.
I try on each and every one.
My favorite is a plaid number in wool,
oranges and reds, soft to the touch.
Then I move to her blouses and jackets
and combine them in surprising ways.

JUNKIE

If she catches me, she'll kill me.
So my heart's pumping
like a bouncing Ping-Pong ball.
I wish I'd managed to find out
where she was going today,
but I am distracted by the historic news
of Gagarin, who beat out all the other candidates.
I'm ready to tackle her shoes.
We have the same size feet
only mine are not ugly.
I look grown-up in high heels.
I trot around the bedroom admiring myself,
a junkie getting her fix.

ICING ON THE CAKE

In honor of Yuri Gagarin,
and turning fifteen of course,
I'm going for the icing on the cake.
I trot into her bathroom,
home to her makeup,
open up drawers,
pull out each little package of blush,
eye shadow, mascara, lipstick.
I love this part, the laying on of her face
on mine.
As if we belonged to each other.

NO TIME

Until.
No!
The jingle of her keys turning!
The front door opening!
Suddenly, I'm the fugitive of daughters,
frantically putting everything away,
cleaning up, hoping to escape from the bathroom
before she arrives.
But I've opened up too many tubes,
compacts, and creams.
My mother's shoes click on the wooden floor
with the precision of an army general.

BIG DAY ON PLANET EARTH

I shove her makeup into the drawers,
leaving colored powder floating over the counters.
"Maisie," she's calling. "Mai-*zie!*"
I'm wiping up the mess, washing my cheeks,
opening the window a slit
so the harsh perfume escapes.
And here's the inevitable, demanding hammering
on the door.
"Maisie, what are you doing
in my bathroom?"
"It's my birthday!
And, uh, Yuri Gagarin is going into space!"
I sputter.
"That's why you're trespassing?"
"Well, I got so excited at this historic moment—
it's a big day on planet Earth.
I guess I gave myself a headache,
so I came in here to find the aspirin,
and then suddenly I had to pee."
I throw myself on the toilet
and manage to aim against the basin
so it's convincingly loud.
"I'll be out in a minute."
"There's aspirin in your bathroom!"
"I couldn't find it, Mom."
I add "Mom" as a desperate measure,
to remind her I am not some fantasy enemy
but her daughter.

NO VISA

She doesn't leave right away,
but the door's locked, so for now I'm safe.
"Sorry," I call out again.
"It was an emergency.
It's a big day on planet Earth," I repeat.
I can imagine her rolling her eyes:
"My daughter is a dingbat."
Finally, I hear her high heels clicking away,
so I finish the cleanup job as best I can,
take out the aspirin bottle
and leave it on the counter
as if I'm forgetful,
flush the toilet.
I'm in her territory, a foreigner
that has no visa to be in her room,
her closet,
or, more importantly,
her life.

STUPID

When I'm done, I open the door.
There she is, arms crossed, feet firmly planted,
eyebrows raised, staring, suspicious eyes.
Oh no!
NO!
This is the moment I realize
I forgot to change out of the last skirt!
I'm still wearing it!
What will happen to me now?
"I figured since it's my birthday, Mom,
you wouldn't mind."
"You figured wrong, girl.
Do you really imagine that
I don't know what you're up to?
Do you think I don't know
that you try on my clothes?
You must think I'm stupid."
"I don't think you're stupid—"
"Clearly, you do. Why are you such a sneak?"
"I don't know," I say hopelessly.
"I will not live with a sneak!"
My face pulses; I don't know what to protect.
So as best I can, I run,
well, gallop down the hallway,
into my room, knees knocking together
in her skinny pencil number.

BE SWEET TO ME

I lock the door and crash onto my bed,
shimmy up against the cool wall
so I can feel something firm
against my feeling-sorry-for-myself body.
Then it comes to me,
the reason I sneak to her closet.
I'm trying to wear my mother.
It's the only way I can get close to her.

I won't stop, either, unless one day,
with the gentlest, kindest
Kleenex-soft fingers,
she kindly brushes my face,
sweeps the hair out of my eyes,
and smiles.
I'll stop this madness when a miracle finally happens,
when she decides to be sweet to me.
That's when I'll no longer envy
the Russian son of a milkmaid
who will float in outer space,
bravely untethered
from this unforgiving Earth,
clearly loved enough
to soar into the darkness, safe in his heart,
convinced he'll return home—
while I am captive in my mother's closet.

JAMES JOYCE AGAIN

Later, I bolt outside with the intention of running
the entire way over to Rachel's.
I hear my name: "Maisie, Maisie . . . !"
"I'm late!" I zip past Richie.
He grabs my arm. "Happy birthday!
James Joyce—"
"James Joyce is dead!" I say flatly.
"Mon dieu! Don't *be* like that, Maisie!
Slow down."
He puts an envelope in my hand.
I decide to stop and open it right there
and read it in front of him:
"'First kiss does the trick.
The propitious moment.
Something inside them goes pop.'
At least you're not writing about death!"
"Girls like kisses better, I've heard!" he says,
smiles so wide—and those *dimples*—!
"I want to try again!"
"Not now, I'm late!"
"Cherie," he says so softly. *"Cherie."*
That word infiltrates my body.
A little flame ignites.
I think to myself,
one day, this skinny, triste boy
might surprise everyone.
Even himself.
Maybe even me.
But now I run.

RATHER STAY HOME

Rachel shows me her new bedspread.
"It's Chinese red!" I say.
"You can't be depressed living inside certain colors:
red, salmon, or even bubblegum pink,"
Rachel explains.
We consider this.
Then we study positive and negative numbers,
listen to music, dance, and try on outfits.
I don't tell her anything about Judith's closet.
Finally, Kiki knocks and says it's time
to visit her studio.
Rachel says, "Go without me.
I was in there for hours yesterday.
Gino came over and we had the best time.
I just want to stay here and paint my nails
and think about it."
So Kiki and I walk down the block,
the wind trying to mess up my hair
as if it were mad at me.
But that just makes me laugh.
I like my hair wild.

THE ART GODS ARE BIG COMEDIANS

Kiki's studio!
Canvases on the wall, the tables, everywhere.
Sketches, crayons, tubes of paints,
linseed oil, stretchers, easels, gesso.
It's a playpen of art.
I inhale the turpentine,

pick up the palette of color.
I'm so attracted to it.
I want to live inside of it.
Kiki doesn't say much,
just lets me wander around.
I ask her about two canvases
she's working on simultaneously.
She says one she really cares about.
The other is just to escape the one
she cares about.
The escape canvas is better,
I think to myself.
"I know," she agrees with my silent assessment.
"It happens a lot.
The more I care, the more I cramp up.
The less I care, the freer I am.
So I always work on two canvases.
Somewhere along the way,
the important canvas may become
the unimportant canvas and vice versa.
The Art Gods are big comedians!"
One day maybe I'll tell Kiki
how I feel about art.
Or show her my work.
Accent on "maybe."

I notice a charcoal drawing tacked to the wall.
It's a torso.
The lines have so much life in them.
The shapes are compelling.
It takes my breath away.
"So did Michelangelo stop by recently?" I ask.

Kiki laughs. "Beautiful, huh?
Rachel did that one!
Once Gino started modeling,
she decided she likes the studio again.
He's magnificent, this new boyfriend of Rachel's."

THIS. NEW. BOYFRIEND. OF. RACHEL'S.

"You'll meet him later," she says.
"He's coming over."
"He's already officially her boyfriend?"
I squeak.
"Oh, honey, don't worry.
Rachel can love more than one person at a time."
"But I want her all to myself!" I blurt out.
"Of course you do!" She laughs.
But I'm not being even a little bit funny.

KEEP THAT TO YOURSELF

Later, Rachel and I share chocolate birthday cake
with her brothers.
Then the door swings open.
A tall, slim boy glides inside
so effortlessly, he might as well be
on ice skates.
"Gino!" Rachel squeals.
Her face blazes as if she's swallowed
a lit-up candle,
not a layer cake.
"Hello, young man," says Kiki,
and she offers him a plate.
He glances in my direction.

Words are suddenly impossible
to form.
He throws a dazzling smile at me;
he shines, this boy.
"You must be Maisie!"
"I must be," I say idiotically.
He grins.
Beautiful mouth. Glistening teeth.
Penetrating eyes. Impossibly long lashes.
Cheekbones from Mongolia
or somewhere in Asia Minor.
James Dean, move over.
He must be the result of a science experiment.
Breaking News: We have created
the perfect textbook specimen
of a human male.
"Relax, Maisie," Rachel says,
as if she can hear me thinking.
"Gino has this effect on people."
I think to myself: As long as this boy
is in the same universe as me,
I will never again relax.

COOL AND ALOOF

I decide to ignore him.
It's better to come off as cool or aloof.
I start thinking, I need to figure out a way
to fall in love with Richie, pronto.
Meanwhile, Gino jokes with Jake and Jonathan.
They clearly adore him.
Finally he leaves and takes my breath
right out the door with him.

Cleaning up, Rachel explains,
"Gino skips a lot of school because he wants to become a model.
I met him in the art store
when I was picking up canvases for Kiki.
He was buying a leather portfolio
to house his photos.
Models need headshots, you know?"
I did not know, but I wasn't going to admit it.
"Isn't he amazing?"
"He's cute," I mumble, I hope dispassionately.
But my voice is weak
and my legs are weaker.

THE MOST HELPFUL THING

Later Kiki collapses on Rachel's bed.
Trying to get my pulse quieted down,
to get myself back to Earth,
I recount the Judith-Macy's-Richie story.
Kiki says straight out, "Your mother's crazy!"
She adds, "Keep that to yourself, honey."

It's the most helpful thing anyone's said to me.
Ever.
But can I really keep it to myself?

Rachel asks Kiki about falling in love.
"How can you tell if it's love, Mom?"
She's using the *L* word?
No! No, no, no!
I'm the one who needs love!
I'm the drowning one!

Kiki says Rachel knows the story:
Kiki fell for Ken
the minute she saw him.
And it's never changed.
They're happy.
Her sentences wander off.
Then she dozes.

I think that even if happiness itself
ever pounded on our front door
and handed Judith and Joe
a lifetime coupon for it,
they wouldn't have stood a chance.
But if happiness ever knocks on my door,
especially if it looks anything
like this boy I just met,
I will jump at it like a drowning girl
reaching for a lifeboat.

TOENAILS

Back home, our very green apartment
is eerily quiet, but Judith's handbag is here.
The kitchen is dark.
There's soup cooling on the stove.
I peek into the master bedroom.
No trace of her.
Then something moves, catching my eye.
Under the bed's dust ruffle,
I spot bright fire-engine-red toenails.
Toenails? I step closer and look down.
That's when I realize my mother's
on her back, lying under the bed,

arms at her sides.
I get on my knees to look.
Her head's almost touching
the bottom of the springs.
Her breasts fall sideways
as if they're running away from each other.
"Mother?"
Her hand shoots out,
grabs my wrist, squeezes it hard,
and digs in with her fingernails.
That's when I know for sure,
his leaving will be my fault.

"Stop! You're hurting me!
Please say something, Mom!"
"Say something?" she growls.
"Here's what I have to say:
You and your bastard father
are the same.
You don't love a thing
that isn't attached to your body."
(But I love so many things, Mother.
You're just not one of them.)

WHO'S WORSE?

Half an hour later, my grandma arrives.
"Your mother doesn't really vant your father to leave,"
she says, pointing to her daughter still under the bed.
"But she refuses to ask him to stay.
Stubborn! Always vas."
She sighs, gets on her knees, and pulls Judith out,
makes her take a shower, sip some soup, swallow a pill.

"Vell, I guess I can't go to Florida yet."
Grandma's a little tan
from sitting on her fire escape,
but underneath, I see white anger.
She tells Judith, with disgust,
that she heard my bastard, cheating father had
dinner with some shiksa from his golf club.
Why did she voice this?
Judith might just crawl back under the bed!

In the kitchen, my grandma fumbles in her purse.
Then she hands me a small box.
A gold filigree bracelet: It fits perfectly.
"I didn't forget your birthday, shana.
I vore this vhen I vas your age."
She smiles with kind eyes.
I swallow down the fullness in me.
Hungarians do not tolerate water-faucet feelings.
"Small wrists like me," she says, sighs.
"I vorry about your mother.
I'm afraid she could snap."
I think, *could?*
"But let's talk about something pleasant, Maisie.
Florida! So beautiful!
I've been going there for years.
Remember vhen Davy, you,
your mom, and I drove down to Miami?
You fell asleep in the back."
"I wasn't asleep," I confess.
"I remember overhearing you
talking about someone named Stan
who didn't want children."
"You shouldn't have listened in,"

she snorts, instantly annoyed.
"You said, 'I admit it, Judith,
it was me who fell for Joe,
just back from the war,
success written across his face
like a Times Square billboard.'
You wanted my mother to marry the 'man
with the neon smile.'
So, Gran, you think my dad has a neon smile?"
Gran sighs.
"I can't believe you're fifteen already."
Then she sips some water
and rubs her arthritic fingers.
I say, "We watched the pink flamingoes
looking proud and sort of silly,
took pictures of the alligators in the Everglades.
And Judith hardly picked on me."
"Oh, Maisie," says Grandma,
"I wish you had thicker skin."
"Me too. But sadly I don't."

The good thing about Gran going to Florida,
which she does nearly every spring,
is that she gives me the key
to her apartment so I can water her plants.
That means a place for me to go.
Quiet.
Alone.
Safe.

TALK TO ME

Davy's finally reappeared.
He's at the piano.
I sit down on the bench next to him.
"Davy, talk to me! Please.
I don't want to be horrible anymore.
I want to be a better sister.
We need each other now."
But he's hiding under heavy protection,
army-tank mode.
He dives back to his chords,
only plays them louder.

Out my window,
I look at the nearly empty baseball field.
Brian O'Neill's throwing Richie a fastball.
Arm high, Richie manages a difficult catch;
the ball makes it into his glove.
Thwap!
Mr. O'Neill runs over, pats
him on the back,
throws his big arms around him
and hugs him tightly.
They twirl around together,
a father-son ballet.
It almost seems impossible:
this beautiful moment
between Richie and his dad.

UNE CLASSIQUE

I go downstairs to watch them,
but when Richie joins me to rest,
he doesn't look happy.
"I'm in so much trouble!
Mrs. Moreau's on the warpath for me.
In Conversational French,
I was sharing about that movie
Breathless. Une classique!" he says.
"Moreau said, '*Vraiment!*'
But then I kept talking. I added
how liberated the French are,
how prudish we Americans can be.
Mrs. Moreau was getting uncomfortable.
But I kept going.
So finally she says, '*Ça suffit,* Richie!
This is not a class about films or social mores;
it's a class to learn
to *speak* the French language!
Comprenez vous?'"

ANIMOSITÉ

"But I was trying to make a point," he says.
"Moreau walks right up to me
and commands me to *va tout de suite*
to the principal's office.
I got up and snapped in my best accent, *'Bien sûr!'*
That's when I made a big mistake.
Un peu de trop! I turned around,
out came: *'Putain. putain!'*"
"What? What's *'putain'*?"
"You don't know what it means?
It means 'whore'!
I swear Moreau had to hold herself back
from slapping me!
She just hates me!"
"You called your teacher a whore?"
"The minute we laid eyes on each other,
it was *animosité*," he says.
"It started in Beginning French.
But yesterday was more like
une guerre gigantesque!
She's going to fail me."
I don't ask, "Why did you do it?"
Because I know why.
I'm the same way, asking for trouble,
as if one kind of trouble
could make another kind of trouble disappear.

MINT IS ANOTHER WORD FOR GREEN

That night after rush hour,
my dad reappears.
This time, when he looks around
at the 100 percent green world,
he says under his breath: "I see."
Then, still wearing his cashmere coat,
he spins around and walks out.
She doesn't try to stop him.
No, she slams the door at his heels.
The entire wall shakes.
So does Davy. So do I.

On Saturday, the painters come again
to work on the hallway outside the elevator.
Light green, this time. Mint.
That's when I know for sure,
that my parents' divorce
is happening sooner, not later.

CLOSET

Outside, a brilliant spring day.
The sun lights up the window shades
and creeps around them, enters my room,
all ready to declare a new season
is on the way.
Then I hear my father's name
and curse words.
Joe, curse word, Joe, curse word.
I dash into their room.
My dad's closet door is wide open.

Inside, it's completely empty!
Bald, naked,
except for one miserable-looking shirt
she bought him that he never wore.
She never seemed to like him,
but she's wailing at the top of her lungs.
Standing by the window, one long phrase
rolling out of her mouth: "*Meehelefmeelefmee.*
Helefme, heleft meeeee.*"
He left me.
That's what she's saying.
But that's not what happened.
What happened is he left *me*!
That bastard left me!
I command the sun to leave us alone.
It's not welcome right now.

MY ENEMY

I run to get my brother.
The world's ending and he's fast asleep!
I wish I were like him,
wish I could push everything away,
but I'm the opposite.
I pull everything into me and it stays there
and gets bigger and stronger
and more dangerous.
I don't know if I should wake Davy
or let him rise on his own.
Crumpled up in his truck sheets,
his hand gripping a plastic truck,
innocent, creamy skin, spiky hair,
one foot dragging on the floor,

he looks so full of possibilities.
It makes me ache
that I think of him as my enemy.
"Davy," I whisper, "wake up!
Something happened."
He mumbles incoherently.
"What? What are you saying, Davy?"
"I know," he whispers.
"I heard him leave."
Then he pulls the pillow over his head
and he's gone again.
But he will wake up.
And he will feel it.
And it will hurt.

THERE FROM THE START

My dad's closet
was always neatly organized;
browns with browns, blues with blues,
shirts, pants, suits, lined up
as if saluting: Here! Present!
Ready to go, go, *go*!
Ready to conquer the world.
Spraying scents on Audrey Hepburn,
who appeared in his perfume commercial.
Being inducted into the Friars Club.
On a yacht with a senator.
But now the worn floor,
where his perfectly shined shoes
stood at attention every morning,
is revealed.

* * *

There's a crack of paint behind where his sportswear
and golf gear once hung.
The only crack I ever noticed
was the one between my parents.
It's as if they never were shiny and new,
as if their fusion was fragile,
as if a fissure was there from the start.
If you touched it, more paint would peel off,
exposing what was underneath,
hard, cold, ugly.

DUMB GAME

Rachel doesn't sound that thrilled
when I call to say
I want to come over again after school.
But when I tell her my dad's gone,
gone for good,
she says, "Of course!"
Then she whispers,
"You know I love you.
You're my bestie.
But Gino will be here . . ."
"I won't stay long, Rache, I promise!"
Gino!
I scold myself:
Do *not* apply layers of mascara!
But I do.
It stains my fingers,
difficult to clean off.
I tell myself:

Do *not* tease your hair,
but then I mess it up so it's slightly wild.
Do *not* put on that blouse that dips low in the front.
But I do that, too.
Eyebrow pencil, shadow,
a touch of blush.
Lipstick blotted.
I check myself out in the mirror.
Gidget meets *La Dolce Vita*.
Have I ever looked better?

I walk fast, whereas if I was smart,
I'd be galloping
in the other direction.
Only trouble can come of this.

Upstairs, Gino emerges from Rachel's front door
into the hallway exactly when I get there.
Hair damp, muscular torso
barely contained in a tight navy tee.
I say hi and throw my eyes
on the floor.
"I'm a little obsessed with drawing him."
Rachel immediately appears.
"You can see why."
He blushes.
I blush, too—at least I feel heat rising in me.
"I can't seem to stop!" Rachel laughs.
"My mother says Gino looks like a painting
in the Museum of Modern Art!"
"The Museum of Modern Art!
We should all go!"
My words are way ahead of my brain.

"Go where?"
Kiki joins us in a paint-covered smock.
"To the Museum of Modern Art!" I say,
pulsing, manic energy taking me over.
"Love that idea!" says Kiki.
"There's a teacher's conference Friday,
so I'm free!
I'll drive us in.
Yes, Rache?"
Rachel shrugs, mumbles an insincere "yes."
"My father just walked out on us,"
I explain to them.
"I'm a little hyper. Sorry.
You should probably ignore me."
Kiki reaches for my shoulder.
But I don't shut up.
"Want to come, Gino?"
This sentence shoots out of my mouth urgently,
as if we were fleeing enemy fire.
"I'm not an artist," he says.
"So what? You're a model!
That counts. Right, Rachel? Tell him!"
"You should come, Gino,"
she mumbles halfheartedly.
"So it's yes, everyone!" I bellow
as if I've personally won the World Series.
As if me being close to my best pal's
drop-dead gorgeous boyfriend
for an entire afternoon
while having the mad hots for him
isn't the worst idea ever.
And the best.

ORIGAMI

It's Friday morning, 7 A.M.,
Kiki kept her word. We're going to New York City!
Getting dressed, I hear deranged shrieking!
It must be a neighbor, or an injured animal?
It's so loud!
I jump out of bed into the cold room.
Was someone knifed?
Murdered?
This is horror movie–type screaming.
I listen hard.
It is very, very nearby, then I realize
it's coming from inside our apartment.
It can't be my mother.
She doesn't get up until ten or eleven.
I shuffle, find my robe,
inch toward the sounds.
What? She's crumpled up on her bedroom floor.
The shrieking is her!
My mother's folded over like origami
and I can't make out much.
I am afraid to do anything
but stand there covering my ears.
I've never heard these sounds before.
There are phrases
but they don't have beginnings
or ends, just wide-open vowels,
almost like something is stuck in her,
something sharp.
I look for blood but there is none.
I don't breathe.
I'm cold. But I'm more than cold.

I only know that this pain she is in
will land on me.
She's snapped.
Danger!
Anything I try to do to help her
will backfire.
I shower, tell Davy to call Gran,
and make my great escape.

LOVE MADE VISIBLE

Later Kiki's Chevy is driving us down the
East River Drive.
I'm in the back seat next to Gino,
hoping my blue eye shadow isn't overkill.
Rachel keeps turning around.
She doesn't trust me.
I don't blame her.
I don't trust me, either.
Kiki is telling us
how long she works on a painting,
how the layers pile up,
how sometimes when she's at it too long,
she loses the whole thing.
How exciting but also frustrating
the process is.
"'Work is love made visible,'" pipes up Gino.
"That's Kahlil Gibran," Rachel adds wisely.
"'And if you cannot work with love
but only with distaste,
it is better that you should leave your work,'"
Gino says grandly.

"I read him at your age, too!"
Kiki laughs dismissively.
I'd love to know more about Gibran.
But not in front of Rachel and Kiki.

We're crossing Central Park,
trees celebrating spring, off-leash dogs, bench sitters, runners,
heading downtown to Fifty-Third Street.
"I love the bustling energy of this city," I say.
"Gibran lived in New York," says Gino.
"Died in New York, too," adds Kiki.
"He was a drunk!"
What's wrong with Kiki? I wonder.

Stoplight at Fifty-Seventh Street.
Three musicians play their violins.
Buses whiz by, cabs; drivers honk at one another.
Everyone's racing somewhere.
The sense I get is that life
is brimming with possibilities.
Inspiring!
I decide to tell Richie later,
"You can have Ireland, my friend.
One day I'll live right smack
in the middle of New York City."
I belong here.

MODERN ART

The museum lobby is open
with lots of light,
especially in the rear.
Since Kiki's a member, (naturally),
we deliver our jackets to the coat room attendant
opposite the information desk.
The long, wide windows look out on the sculpture garden.
"Gaston Lachaise." Rachel points to a statue
of a monumentally huge, shapely woman.
"And there's a Modigliani."
She links her arm through Gino's.
"What do you think?" she asks him.
"'Beauty is eternity gazing at itself in a mirror,'"
he whispers to her.
I think about that.
"Maybe that's why I'm such a slave to beauty,"
I say, catching up with them.
"This is something I worry about."
Rachel turns her back to me.
"Gibran?" Kiki asks.
"Do you really find him that helpful, Gino?"
Oh! Kiki doesn't like Gino!
"Say something my mother can understand,"
prods Rachel.
"I'm glad to be here." Gino flashes
his dazzling smile as if it's a magic trick.
And it is.

"To me, the greatest thing about being an
artist," says Kiki, "is to be able to enjoy
what other people are doing and notice it
in detail that, I'm guessing, civilians miss."
Nope. She doesn't like Gino at all.

PLENTY TO TRANSFORM

I see paintings by Bosch and Grosz.
So compelling and intense,
it makes me believe
they had no choice *but* to paint.
Rachel and Gino take a guided tour
through the collections,
while Kiki does some sketches of the masters.
I wander over to another room
so I can concentrate,
which means being out of sight
of Rachel's boyfriend.
The Degas dancers knock me out.
Every gesture is full of truth,
the painterly tutus,
the poses, the elongated necks, torsos.
The dusty light makes me want to point
my own arched foot.
I once took ballet.
I think:
Degas is telling us
this is where you find heaven.
I gallop ahead, a maniac for art.

HIDE-AND-SEEK

A large canvas stops me in my tracks.
It's called *Hide-and-Seek*.
There's a tree that centers the picture.
In that tree there are large heads with faces
that look like children's.
In the middle is the back of a girl,
then on the bottom, a newborn is emerging.
It has an ambiguous, mystical fairy-tale quality,
The description says this is about the game of Life.
This painting seems like a living thing to me.
It tells me that childhood is fantastic, scary.
I already know that.
The artist, Tchelitchew, has me rooted
in front of his artwork
as if it's transmitting experience
directly into my brain.
I'm glued to the floor.
The crowds must circle around me.
I call out, "Rachel . . ."
"Oh, yeah." She waltzes over holding Gino's arm.
"This is everyone's first favorite."
Gino doesn't move, either.
We're both still, tied to it as if with a tether.
I am tied to him, too.
I have to walk away,
so I feign interest in another artist.
But this is a lie.

Downstairs we all hit the museum store
at the same time.
I buy a postcard of *Hide-and-Seek*.
Gino stands behind me to buy one, too.

I have to keep myself from leaning into him,
a tilted, lusty Tower of Pisa.
Rachel appears, plants herself next to him.
"You two are such beginners,"
she chides.
"Buying the obligatory Tchelitchew.
And the Renoir. So cute!"

ESCAPING

Chugging along on the East River Drive
in heavy traffic,
heading for the Triborough Bridge,
everyone's quiet.
Kiki flicks her cigarette out the window.
Gino grabs Rachel's hand
in the front seat.
She giggles happily.
Finally I say,
"I love that artists get to live inside
their dreams and imaginations
instead of crummy reality."
"That's what Kiki does,"
says Rachel.
"Between being covered in oil paint
and drinking, she escapes every day,
right, Mom?"
"Are you picking a fight
with your mother?" Gino asks.
"After this great trip?"
"Thank you, Gino!" says Kiki.
Rachel mumbles "no." And "sorry."

I see Kiki wink at Gino
through the rearview.
He's on top of his parent game,
that's for sure.

I take out my Tchelitchew postcard
and stare.
Try to get my mind off
this living, breathing work of art
sitting right next to me.

SABBATH

Another Friday night.
The pristine white tablecloth
is laid out with our gold-trimmed china,
candles everywhere;
the newly painted room's dressed up like royalty.
My mother must have taken a tranquilizer
and apologized to her mother,
because they light the candles,
recite the blessing together
with lace handkerchiefs
resting on their heads.
Barukh atah Adonai,
Eloheinu Melekh ha'olam.
asher kid'shanu b'mitzvotav
v'tzivanu l'hadlik ner shel Shabbat.

Grandma, dressed in her pearls
and sensible low-heeled pumps,
has made matzo balls.
When it comes to Grandma's

life-giving soup,
celery, carrots, garlic, and cilantro
float next to luscious pieces of chicken,
and a brisket cools off in the kitchen.
I don't mind being a Jew.

JUST FOR A MOMENT

Nobody glances over
at my dad's empty seat,
but his absence is a presence.
Davy's playing the piano,
lying low.
Outside, the streets are unusually quiet.
Peace has broken out in Parkchester,
at least for a few minutes
in this breezy, almost warm April evening.
I breathe in, as if, for just a moment,
I can inhale the blessing,
the oneness, the harmony, and—
Dad or no Dad—
the sacredness of the Sabbath.

ANTI-GOD

Why I make trouble, I do not know.
"Mom, why do so many religions
believe that God has a thing about hair?"
I ask.
"Devout Jewish women
have to wear wigs.
The Amish have beards
and wide-brimmed hats.

Muslim women cover up with
hijabs.
As if hair—which grows on all of us—
is somehow a sin.
Even the Pope has a skull cap,
and it's hot in Italy!
The God I imagine
doesn't care about hair.
I mean, He's not a beautician!"

SHE'S A THINKER

"See how she is, Mom?"
Judith complains,
as if I were cursing.
"She does have a mouth on her!"
my grandma chirps proudly,
and winks at me.
"She's a *thinker*, Judith!"
My mother is silent.
"I really am curious," I say.
"Maybe if you explain things to me,
I won't be practically anti-God.
Because this holy deity created tuberculosis,
polio, famine, and genocide.
He created nasty mosquitoes,
which carry disease!
People are born missing organs.
But, somehow, covering *hair*
is one of His main priorities?
I don't get it!"
"Maisie needs to go to Hebrew school,"
my grandma whispers.

"She needs to understand God."
But the word *God*
tends to make Judith snort.
So I'm safe.
She'll never send me there.

MUMBLE, MUMBLE

Mother and Grandma have begun
to speak in Hungarian, *Igen, nem, igen.*
I recognize a few words.
Mumble, mumble.
Sounds like a language
a kindergartner made up.
I doodle on my drawing pad
while I wait for them to finish.
My pencil dances. I study them
and realize they both have the same nose,
eyebrows, hands, and long fingers,
only Grandma's have blue veins,
old hands, very old.
But she doesn't use them
to hurt anyone.
I wonder if she ever did.

GO EASIER

What was my grandma Ruth
like as a mother?
Did her soft gray eyes ever harden?
After dessert I show her the drawing
I did of her in profile.
"She captured me perfectly!" she exclaims.
She turns to her daughter.
"Judith, look at this!
Can't you go a little easier
on your talented brown-eyed girl?"

BEFORE I WAS BORN

"You're her grandmother,
I'm her mother! It's different!"
Judith sips her wine.
My grandmother takes my hand
and Judith's, holds them to her heart
as if comforting two toddlers.

SHE WAS A MODEL

"Maisie, do you want to hear
about your mom's life
before you were born?"
"I do!" I say. "Tell me!"
I pray there's a version of her
I could like.
"She was a model,
strutting the showrooms on Seventh Avenue."
My grandmother urges my mother to speak.
"Tell her, Judith!"
"Well, I was a perfect size six!"
Judith's eyes become luminous.
"You can't believe how tedious
the fittings were.
There were endless alterations
under hot wool winter coats.
But I loved every minute,
seeing men's eyebrows raise up,
admiring us in our designer jackets,
tailored tight skirts.
My world was imported fabrics,
chiffon from France,
silk from India,
the finest Italian merino.
I had the most elegant neck,
the longest legs, the smallest waist."
She stands up with her hands on her hips
to show us she still has a great figure.

THE PRETTIEST

Davy appears.
"I bet you were the prettiest, Mom,"
he says on cue.
That was my line!
Davy's a little Machiavelli!
"I was! Until I got pregnant."
Pregnant crawls out of her mouth
like a curse word.
"So while my girlfriends
pranced around showing off
their sample chiffon cocktail dresses
that floated around them like a cloud—
which they got to wear to the Waldorf
at cocktail hour and listen to the big bands
and drink Bloody Marys with promising young men—
I had to stay home!
My glory days were over.
Maisie was colicky,
screaming for something
I couldn't give.
I was only twenty-three.
My need, her need, no contest."

My grandmother's eyebrows furrow.
Davy stands behind Judith and
rubs her shoulders.
Naturally, she pats his hand.

IT'S FOR YOU

Our phone rings and rings.
My father's been trying us for days.
I refuse to take his calls.
Judith grabs it, screams into it:
"Leave them alone, Joe!"
Slam!
But it rings on and on.
I hate that sound. I pick it up.
My dad says hi as if we're pals.
"Once I thought I had a father,
but now I realize
you're just some stranger's boyfriend,
not a father at all,
nobody I want to know. Ever!"
This time *I* slam it down.
Who's worse,
a mother who unabashedly detests you
or a father who swears he adores you
but treats you as if you're someone
he might have seen on a bus?

I NEED YOU

I'm so glad to escape
and return to school Monday.
Rachel's been chosen to chair
the decorations committee
for the spring dance.
As we walk through the hallways,
she grabs my arm.
"You have to help, Maisie!"
I shake my head doubtfully.
"Look, I wish, truly wish, your dad
was still around
and that he wasn't a jerk
and that your mother wasn't a bitch
and that you weren't so glum—"
"Well, they are and I am!"
"But you have to co-chair the committee
with me anyway! I need you!"

"I'm not . . . See . . . I can't . . .
Divorce is a little overwhelming."
Rachel stops walking.
"Divorce? Are you sure?"
That *D* word hangs there.
My eyes gaze out the window at the misty clouds.
The air is greenish,
like my least favorite Jell-O.
I say, "Air is Jell-O.
I can hardly breathe."
"I hate breathing Jell-O!" Rachel says.
"Especially the orange kind."

"The yellow is worse," I counter.
I'm relieved to joke a little.
Then she hugs me tightly right there
in front of the display case in the hallway,
housing papier-mâché art projects
and announcements for band practice
and awkward photographs of the faculty
looking overworked, pasty,
and not remotely content.
I feel kind of lucky.

RABBIT HOLE

Rachel talks about the theme.
"It should be a celebration of democracy," she says.
"We could all dress like White House personnel."
I tease, "I don't think anyone wants to wear
business clothes to a dance, Rachel.
Except you. You mostly want to wear a hat and
dress as Jackie Kennedy.
You're such a Kennedy freak!
I'm glad everyone voted for the theme to be *West Side Story*."
"*When you're a Jet, you're a Jet all the way . . .*"
she sings.
Neither one of us can carry a tune.
"Rache, it took genius Jewish guys
Sondheim, Bernstein,
Laurents, and Robbins
to write a musical starring Puerto Rican gangs.
I know this because of Davy,
our local music prodigy."
"See, you *get* it, Maisie!
You have to change your mind!

Seriously if you're not careful
you'll slide down the rabbit hole
along with your family.
You're already halfway there.
Decorating for the dance is the ideal solution."
Her enthusiasm fills me
with a little bit of optimism.
But I don't say yes.
"Gino might help out." She smiles
with those haunting green eyes.
Then she pulls a *Life* magazine out of her pocket.
It's got photos of Carol Lawrence
and Larry Kert.
"This is my inspiration for the posters of the Jets.
You do the Sharks!"
I'm groaning no.
But I'm also looking to see if I can spot
Gino in the art room,
and sure enough, he emerges out of the supply closet.
"What's he doing here?"
I ask, sounding almost harsh.
"I told you! Helping!" she says. "Why not?"
Rachel tells me what to do,
then she's busy flirting.
She should be flirting.
Gino's *her* boyfriend.
I love her.
She deserves to be happy.
So I paint. Before I know it,
long bursts of color stick under my fingernails.
Paint splotches are in my hair
and covering my clothes:
Cadmium Yellow, Alizarin Crimson, Burnt Umber.

And, I lose, at least for a little while,
the part of me that's broken.
By the end of the week,
We've sprayed graffiti on huge boards,
creating an empty lot.
We've dragged in a basketball net,
done a sketchy rendition
of the highway overhead,
just like in the musical.
The gym's transformed.
I'm transformed, too,
back into being a member
of the human race.
But not even close to being over
this stupid, stupid crush.

I'M A MONSTER

Home.
The house is a tenebrous Edward Hopper still life.
My mother sits in the dark,
eating potato chips.
Only potato chips.
She's closed the curtains.
Wears no makeup, nor slippers,
nor shoes.
Her lips are dry.
Her hair is dirty.
She looks like a drawing you might see
in the dictionary for depression.
Only her version can turn violent.
So no way I'm staying here.
"I need pretzels," I announce.

"Nobody needs pretzels," says Davy.
I give him a sullen look.
Judith rasps, "Go to Safeway and get
some onions and tomatoes and more potato chips
and take David with you"
in her "do not dare argue" voice.

Davy ambulates slowly.
Is this on purpose, to annoy me?
"C'mon! Put on your jacket already, Davy!"
"Okay, okay."
He's so easygoing.
I'm so hard-going.
"Where are your glasses, kid?"
Now my voice is shrill.
He opens his big brown eyes,
mumbles, "It's hard to be me
when you're angry at me."
That makes me get a grip on my nasty self.

NO POETRY HERE

At the Oval, Richie O'Neill falls in with us
on his way to pick up his paycheck.
"The Safeway smells of cardboard
and overripe fruit!" he says.
"There's no poetry there."
"Of course there's no poetry
at the Safeway!" I laugh.
"I think I'll try to write a Safeway poem
anyway," he says.
"I believe art is everywhere.
Just think of James Joyce."

"Nobody thinks of Joyce
as much as you do, Richie!"
He gives me significant eyes.
"Art's everywhere, Maisie.
You should know that; you're an artist."
"I'm artsy, but I'm not an artist,"
I correct him.
"*Tu es grandement doué*,"
he says, winks.
Gifted!
His words make me quiver.
Does he really think that?

AWASH IN SQUASH

The Safeway smells of bananas.
Davy drifts off to the cookie aisle.
Richie takes my hand
and leads me to the cereals,
way in the back of the store.
"We don't need cereal!" I protest.
"You need this!" He plants a wet kiss on me.
I push him away.
"I thought you *wanted* to be kissed!"
he complains.
"Not in the grocery store!
Not just any time!"
I don't say, not you, not anymore.
Because my first erotic encounter
no longer has your name on it.
"Wow. You're complicated, Maisie."
He heads to the office to collect his paycheck.

Davy finds me and hands me three Hershey bars.
I get pretzels, onions, tomatoes, potato chips; pay and pray
I haven't forgotten anything.
Richie reappears and walks us home.
"I'm saving every cent I make.
I'm going to have a future!" he announces.
"That's the point of being a teenager,
isn't it?" asks Davy.
"Having a future?"
My brother of few words has actually spoken.

MUSHY

On the way home,
Davy points to a window that's been smashed.
"Some idiot Paddies
broke into the kosher bakery.
One had a gun!" Richie says.
"It's the bad Irish. They embarrass me."
I think of my grandmother's cooking.
"I bet if those rapscallions had her linzer tortes,
they'd change their mind about the Jews," I say.
"And if everyone read James Joyce,
they'd love the Irish," says Richie.
The groceries are heavy, and he carries them
without complaining.
At our street, I thank him.
He looks all proud, puts the bags down,
and grips my hands in his,
then sticks another piece of crumpled paper
into my jacket pocket
and trots off to his own building.

"Richie O'Neill has a crush on you,"
says Davy matter-of-factly.
"No, he *doesn't*, Davy!"
I say with too much volume.
"He's teaching me about poetry!
And sad onions. It's very cool."
"Then why are you upset?
Don't you think he's cute?" Davy asks.
I stare at him. "What do you mean?"
"It doesn't matter," he says.
I didn't know guys
knew which guys were cute.
"He's probably a little desperate,
hormones and all," he adds,
wise beyond his years.
I am thinking I don't know my brother.
"It's normal," Davy adds philosophically.
"The body is changing.
I see how you look at boys.
I see how boys look at you.
Like you're in heat."
"Who asked you, Davy?" I'm astounded.
"Well, Richie O'Neill definitely
has a crush on you,"
he says again, and picks up his pace.

NO BRATS

Still in her silk robe,
my mother trots around menacingly.
"Cut up the onions, you ungrateful brat."
I feel the need to explain:
"Ungrateful brats don't help people.
That's what makes us brats!"
"I can't handle your back talk.
I'm at my wit's end," says Judith.
"I'm at my wit's end, too!"
I say. "Maybe you should hit me.
Let off some steam."
She doesn't hit me.
She throws a pan at the wall.
It crashes on the linoleum.
"That belonged to my grandmother Estelle,
who gave it to Grandma Ruth.
Now it's dented, Maisie!"
"If you didn't want it dented, Mother,
why'd you throw it?"
I sprint into my bedroom.

PLATES

Clanging, clattering, this time
as if in some kind of unhinged concert,
a demented duet
comes from Richie's building again.
Plates, one after the other,
crash, splatter onto the sidewalk.
I look toward the O'Neills' floor.
It's entirely lit up.
Shadows cross behind the window shades
quickly, as if in a silent movie, a
hostile two-step.
I think of Richie wondering what to do,
knowing he can't really do anything.
For some reason,
it's Richie's hopeless family fights
that break me down and make me weep.

HEBREW SCHOOL

Even though she doesn't go to temple—
not even on the High Holy Days—
Judith's decided that being at her wit's end
means I belong in Hebrew school.
Probably for the rest of my life.
(And during spring vacation!)
The only time *she* uses the word *God*,
is when she screams "goddamnit."
In retrospect,
she believes failing to force me
to have a bat mitzvah was tragic.
She thinks it's not too late;
she's banking that a Jewish education
will fix me right up.
"I'm fifteen now!" I holler.
"Nobody starts Hebrew school at fifteen!"
"You do!" she says.

Next thing I know,
I'm the oldest student,
sitting in the back of the fourth-floor classroom
in sour-smelling Temple Emanuel,
staring at the wall clock,
whose hands refuse to move.

THE JEWISH GOD

Rabbi Shiffman lectures us about
the Jewish God, Adonai.
He warns us that even though the Supreme Being
is incredibly busy,
He's always watching us,
mostly disapproving.
According to the rabbi,
by the time you wake up in the morning,
you've probably already done something awful.
Which, in my case,
according to Judith, is true.
I don't like this God—smiting
seems to be His specialty—
but Judith likes Him fine.
Which makes sense.
They have so much in common.

THE BACK OF THINGS

As Rabbi Shiffman drones on,
I'm drawing people's heads,
boys' hair under yarmulkes,
necks, ponytails, profiles.
I like a big nose or a small chin
(better to draw one than to have one).
I'm getting to be an expert
at rendering the backs of things.
Eventually I'm staring at the trees outside.
Their leaves are a Cézanne palette.
There's a mild rustle of wind.
One leaf drifts down.
I want to fall with it,
out of the stifling, boring,
monotone lectures and onto the neatly cut grass.
I want to lie there and get damp
and smell the season,
think about my father.
I miss him, especially around nine at night.
That's when we had talks.
He was interested in me.
He got my jokes.
He had wisdom about people—
except for Judith.
"Nobody can really understand her."
That's what he told me.

But I'll never talk to him again.
Maybe I'll just die here,
instead of having to sit
on this hard wooden chair
learning about eons of persecution.

THE MAPLE TREE

When the rabbi dismisses us,
I bolt out of temple
while the other kids discuss the Torah.
Outside two of the Irish boys
I've seen around make an appearance.
They both have pomaded curly red hair.
Garrison belts are threaded through their dungarees
and look like they could be used
as emergency weapons.
They casually toss cigarette butts
onto the scraggly lawn with only clumps of new grass.
Laughing, they approach me,
suddenly pin me against the trunk of the maple tree that stands
between the temple
and the street.
One puts his large rough hand
over my mouth,
the other unbuttons my jacket,
lifts up my blouse.
His calloused paw,
under my bra, grabs my naked chest.
"You people killed Jesus our Savior!"
he shouts.
I writhe and scream, too,
but almost no sounds come out.
Again, they laugh, faces redder than
the velvet ruby seats in the chapel.
These auburn-haired, freckle-faced bullies
squeeze my chest hard and it hurts.
I try to bite their fingers,
but they only enjoy the moment more.
Under my blouse, my breasts shrivel.

Nobody has ever touched them
besides me.
I don't think Jesus would approve of this
and this Jewish God I've heard so much about
isn't helping, either.
But I never expected Him to.

I CAN'T BE REAL TO HER

Finally they leave.
I fall against the tree,
try to feel my feet again.
I duck my head down and hug myself, refusing to cry.
Then I force myself into action.
I sprint past the tall apartment buildings,
in their dirty, white-brick uniforms,
then the gas station, where every single car
needs a wash,
then the Oval Fountain.
Richie O'Neill, sitting in his usual spot,
sees me, asks, "What are you doing here?"
I fake being normal.
"Don't you ever go home, Richie?"
I sound mean.
But then, before I know it,
I blurt out what happened
except I don't say where they touched me.
Richie says he bets it was
Timmy O'Hara and Billy McDonald,
jumps up, swears to knock them out.
I cross my arms.
"You *can't*, Richie,
they're twice your size!

They'll use your head for a punching bag.
You're nice, but don't be stupid!"
"I am nice," Richie says.
"Only nobody seems to notice."
"I notice!" I protest.

Then at the turnoff
I leave him, hustle into our building.
Inside the apartment, I don't say a word.
My mother will find a way to make it my fault.
I wish she would make it their fault,
but I can't chance it,
so I wash my breasts as if they were little children
that somebody hurt.
I can't let her know how much
I don't like her God, her temple,
or those boys.

FLIRTING

If there ever was a grandma moment,
this would be it. I dial her.
"Bubelah! I'm so glad it's you!
I svear, your great-aunt Dalvinka
is driving me crazy!" she whispers.
"Today, vhen ve vent out for lunch,
she insisted on talking to every single person
of the male persuasion.
Can you imagine this old lady flirting?
She flicks those electric-blue-eye-shadow eyes on the men.
She doesn't realize that makeup
cakes up on old lids.
And that bright-pink lipstick is not appropriate!
She's not a teenager!
Vey!" Grandma finally takes a breath.
"Sorry, doll. That's not why you called.
So talk, darling."

NO NAZIS

"I was at Temple Emanuel," I begin.

"I don't like it there.

It's not . . . safe."

"Vhat are you saying?

Dank Gott, the Nazis are gone!"

"I'm not talking about the Nazis!"

"Bubelah, is someone being rude to you?"

"Yes, Grandma, in a way . . . very . . ."

My voice teeters.

"Vell, then, you put them in their place

with that sharp mouth of yours.

You're not shy!"

"It wasn't what they said, Grandma . . ."

"Hold on, bubelah . . ."

"Yes, Dalvinka," she whispers,

"I certainly *do* vant to finish the game!

Don't you dare touch a card!"

She comes back on the phone.

"Maisela, I'm so glad you called.

But I'm not letting your great-aunt vin so fast!

Let's talk again soon!"

The phone clicks.

The line goes dead.

THERAPY TONES

So I dial Rachel.
Kiki picks up.
I can tell from her voice, if I say anything,
no matter how she responds
in her low, rumbly, therapy tones,
I'll start sobbing.
I can't afford that.
I hang up, will myself to take a nap.
Maybe I'll dream about a place of peace.
I drift off, but police sirens
blast me awake again.
Sometimes the Bronx
feels like a Fourth of July firecracker,
as if everyone always has a good reason to explode.

HOW RATTLED I AM

The nap did nothing to erase how rattled I am.
My blouse is so wet from crying
that my hair sticks to my chin.
The streetlights aren't on yet,
but there's a moon flickering
behind Richie's building,
teasing through clouds,
looking like the cover
of a horrifying mystery novel.
My toes have cramped,
so I get up slowly and hobble around my bedroom,
sure that nothing that can happen tonight
will soothe me.

I dial Rachel's again.
"Gino's here!" she mumbles urgently.
"We're alone!
You get what I'm saying?!
Gotta go!"

I look through my curtains.
Richie's bedroom is fully lit.
I run to the elevator, cross the grassy knoll
that separates our buildings,
bound up his stairs,
knock firmly at his door,
relieved I don't hear any yelling from inside.
He opens it looking scruffy.
Then, a thought captures him.
Maybe a thought about me.
His gaze becomes immediately present.
Seeing him so concerned
makes me start blubbering.
I tell him exactly where those boys touched me.
This makes me start sobbing.
Which turns into howling.
Richie reaches for my hand.
"Poor Maisie," he mumbles.
His eyes get watery.
"I can't believe this!" I shout.
"You're crying! You ruined it!"
I retrieve my hand,
turn around, head down the hallway,
and pound the elevator button.
He calls, "What did I ruin?
I'm just feeling what you're feeling!"
"Not *helpful*!" I yell.

I don't explain why kindness kills romance for me.
Because I don't know why it does.

The elevator door opens.
I dash inside.
There's a woman and her young son.
I bark, "Stop looking at me!"
The boy wilts.
I mumble, "Sorry."
And promise myself I'll stop being such a jerk.

OUT LOUD

My grandmother has come over
to knit with her daughter.
I set the table.
In between counting stiches, she says:
"Vell, no doubt, Joe's a skirt-chaser!"
Ever since my dad left,
she's often here, hovering.
"Vich is vhy I varned you, Judith,
not to make him feel as if every time
he valked into the house
he vas on probation."
Now my mother's yelling
at her mother.
"I knew you'd blame me that he left.
Out loud, you call him names,
but under your breath
you whisper,
'It's all your fault, Judith!'
Ever since you gave my brother
the scissors when I was five,

which he swung at my left eye
blinding it,
you've been hard on me.
You're still mad for all the trips
to the eye doctor.
I remember, sitting in the subway,
you gripped my hands,
holding them tightly because
what you probably wanted
was to let them go.
But you must know that
no decent mother,
whose son was sent home from school
with an 'attitude problem'
and who was jealous of his baby sister,
would allow him to play
with scissors before dinner,
when he was always at his crankiest."

CRYING IS LIKE A PRAYER

I fold the last napkin thinking
how embarrassed
my mother's always been about her limited vision.
How I never even knew the story.
I close my left eye so I can feel sorry for her.
It only lasts a second.
She snaps at me to stop lollygagging.
I must retreat
before hell breaks loose.
I spy on Judith's face, mouth in a hard scowl,
eyebrows almost meeting at the nose.
I picture living inside a small bank safe

without a key.
That's the country Judith resides in.
It has to be lonely.
At some point, she must have decided
she would not feel her sorrows.
I wish I could tell her
that her heart is like a target
with a quiver of arrows
shot through the red center.
It makes me sad.
If I were her, I'd find a private place,
somewhere kind of beautiful,
and let myself go.
Sometimes crying is like a prayer.

PEACE OFFERINGS

I remember how Leslie always said,
"If you are an artist,
you have a gift.
Gifts have to be given."
An urge comes over me;
I'm running to my sketch pad.
As if anyone, let alone me,
could rescue Judith.
I tear out a drawing of her rosebush on the balcony.
In a change-of-heart moment, I show it to her.
"What do you think of this, Mom?"
I dare not tell her what Kiki said—
that I have talent.
She says: "A peace offering?"
Then, remarkably, she becomes quiet.
And looks, really looks.

"That's—lovely!"
She garbles her surprise.
It's as if my drawing reaches her
in a way I never can.
Maybe that's what talent is?

After the last piece of rugelach is gone,
I appeal to my grandma.
"I can't go back to that temple," I say.
Before my mother can speak, Grandma Ruth says, "I agree. You
can't go back."
And then she leaves.
I retreat into the bathroom,
run the water, sit in the tub,
and take my own advice.
I breathe and let my chest open up.
I repeat it several times.
That's how I get the temple
to disappear down the drain
along with the bath salts;
so I manage
not to turn myself into a clenched-up,
muscle-bound boulder of a girl,
tight, angry, resistant.
After a while, the water cools,
my skin puckers.
I towel off, put on my soft pajamas,
and whisper sweet things
to my sad self.

YUCK!

After school, Rachel and I take turns
sketching each other's costumes
for *West Side Story*. Rachel says,
"At least Judith doesn't try
to be your sister!"
She says she's tired of Kiki's confidences,
tired of knowing the details
of her parents' marriage.
"Yuck! I keep telling her,
Mom, please! Not interested!
But you know Kiki.
She's so immature!
She wants to be one of us."

CAT BURGLAR

In our mailbox there's another
self-serving letter from Joe
full of ridiculous poetic flourishes,
as if he were some late-blooming beatnik.
Allen Ginsberg. Lawrence Ferlinghetti.
As if bad poetry is going to make us like him more.

Dear Maisie and Davy,
None of this is your fault.
You must never think it was.
Try to understand
I was not brought up
to run away in the night
like a cat burglar,
waiting to pack my things,

anticipating my freedom
as if I were a convict,
desperate to have the prison gates
clang open at long last.
I hoped that once I was gone,
your mom would begin
to see you as something more
than pawns in our marriage.
You can blame me for how I left
but not for wanting to find love again.
I've never been sneaky,
but as the sun teased up that dawn,
sneaking is exactly what I did.

DELUSIONAL

If my father thinks that writing boneheaded notes
is going to change my mind,
he's delusional.
Well, he must be delusional
to have made the promises
during those special "it's me and you,
Maisie" conversations we had
and then suddenly fly the coop.
Did it ever occur to him
that I've had enough rejection
to last a lifetime?
No, it didn't; *I* didn't occur to him.

I ask Rachel if I can sleep over.
I still haven't told her about temple.

SISTER/MOM

For once, Gino isn't there!
That night, as Rachel and her brothers
walk the dog, Kiki and I keep talking.
She's not afraid of being honest!
Adults have inner lives and struggles!
If this is what it's like
having a sister/mom, I like it.
Until Kiki says, "One of these days,
you should talk to your dad, Maisie.
Don't you miss him?"
I think how much I miss him.
But not the version that ran off
without even explaining.
I miss the old version.
I wish I had a way to be with that dad.
I wish I could call him
and time would run backward.
And he'd be beating me in Ping-Pong,
sending me a killer serve.
At home.
Ready to laugh at my jokes.

I change the subject, ask Kiki about her art.
She points to a sketch on the wall:
"Don't you feel like you could swim
in those colors naked?
This is the palette of les Fauves.
Doesn't it make you want to sing?"
I *do* feel exactly the same way!
I whisper to myself, "Les Fauves."

PSYCHE

She hums a Greek folk song,
like Melina Mercouri,
who won Best Actress at Cannes
for *Never on Sunday.*
We talk about the "psyche" (Greek word!),
which she's learning about
in grad school.
Kiki says I'm deep, like her,
and you only get deep
because circumstances force you to grow.
So that's when I tell her
about being felt up.
She hugs me tenderly.
That gets me crying.
Rachel returns and crawls into the bed.
They both stroke my shoulder.
It's sweet but almost unbearable.
Those boys stole from me.
I can never get back what they took.

WORRYING

I'm swaying on the groaning IRT,
on my way to my grandmother's.
I wish she'd ask about me
instead of talking so much.
Good luck, Maisie, I think.

When I get to her place,
she puts a slice of Bundt cake on a plate.

It's moist, lemony, glazed.
I defy anyone to resist it.
I don't.
She pours me a glass of milk.
"So stop looking so perplexed
and tell me, vhat's new vith you?"
Finally!
"I'm worrying," I tell her.
"At your age, vorrying is optional,"
she says flatly.
"Not for me.
I've always been worrying."
The next question should be,
"Vhy? Tell me!"
Instead she says:
"Things vill get better, honey,
I promise."
Well, this was a useless visit.
She must know it, because then she hands me
the address of Womrath's Book Shop.
"I have a charge there.
Go buy yourself an art book, shana, darling.
Something to make you happy."
I'm guessing this means she realizes
she's not that great at being there for me.

I BOUGHT A BOOK

I'm on the bus to Fordham Road,
with my grandmother's charge
I'll buy the Pavel Tchelitchew biography.
Rachel made sure

I knew his painting *Hide-and-Seek*
is a cliché because so many teenagers fall for it.

She told me:
"As we leave our tender youth behind,
the canvas offers one last
terrifying glance backward
to remind us what we survived.
There's the back of a girl
disappearing into this phantasmagoria.
You get it, right?"
I shudder thinking about it.
"It's scary. Like childhood."
Like my childhood, anyway.
This art is horrific and fantastical.
I love it.

Tchelitchew was Russian and grew up
studying art and ballet,
like me!
And he thought about hell!
Like *me*!
He loved men, not women.
Like Davy.
But who cares who Pavel loved?
Artists have an independent streak!
They have to.
I surely do.
I'm not sure about Davy.
But he's going to have to develop one,
that's for sure.
Judith says I'm going to hell.
I'll be put there for my rage,

Pavel will be there for his daring.
I'll recognize him even if
he doesn't recognize me.

I find the book at Womrath's.
The cover's a little dusty.
I suppose it's been
sitting on the shelf too long,
but I buy it, slip it into my school bag,
and button up again,
hurry toward the bus stop.
It's darker now at five o'clock.
I want to get home for meatloaf dinner,
one dish even my mother can't murder.
Then I can read and escape Judith's
inevitable lecture about how awful my father,
Joe, is for leaving.
And the way he left, such a coward,
disappearing in the middle of the night,
stealing our sense of security,
robbing our future.
I wish I could tell her
her words only make everything worse.
And let's face it.
It was you, Mother, he was fleeing.
She will eat, cursing her lawyer,
then wash the dishes as if she's trying
to scrub the patterns off them.
But tonight I will disappear
into my brand-new purchase.
It invites me into a world I belong to.
Or will.
One day I, too, will be a painter.

My dad might be gone,
but Pavel is waiting! (I call him that now.)

But on the way from Womrath's to the bus stop,
I pass the other, newer bookstore.
Classical music drifts out onto the street.
Maybe Mozart?
I smell fresh cinnamon tea.
I imagine the soft down-filled chairs inside
and the free cookies on the table
near the toasty, blazing fireplace.
I go in, eat a gingersnap, wander around,
then discover the same exact art book
I just bought!
Only this cover is bright and shiny.
This brand-new book is meant for me.
It's full of promise,
and I need to find promise in my life.
I slip it into my school bag,
place the Womrath copy
on the shelf in its stead,
head out again.
I am not stealing!
Technically, I'm no thief.
I'm nothing like my dad.

Night approaches as if in a big hurry
It's a race between me and the blackening sky—
temperatures dipping, breeze whipping up.
I walk fast, but my bag is heavy.
Or is that my conscience?
My steps slow down.
Gravel in my stomach.

I begin to consider; in a way,
I have stolen a book!
I do have a larcenous streak!
But, I tell myself, nobody will guess.
Nobody could possibly find out.
And the store can still sell that dusty copy
to someone else who loves Tchelitchew, too.

Except my mother will know.
She'll take one look at me
and as if I'm made of cellophane,
she'll know everything.
The only thing she can't see about me
is my hurting heart.
And what will I say?
I'll be in trouble, big trouble,
bad trouble, trouble, trouble.
The bus finally approaches.
The doors swing open.
Then close.
But the young thief watches
as it rumbles away.
She returns to the store, feeling her cold toes,
wind at her neck,
fear in her heart,
compelled to exchange the shiny new copy
for the dusty one.
Lest a crime be revealed.
And a criminal.

So instead of imagining how Tchelitchew
is going to lead me into speaking a new language
and a new glorious, promising painterly future,

I'm thinking about what it's like
to be a crook,
thinking one crook in a family is enough.

Finally, I'm sitting on the stuffy,
overheated bus groaning up the hill,
wishing I could be an innocent again.
My mother (the one I dream about),
would laugh and say things like
"you take yourself too seriously."
Or "I understand."
Or "you did the right thing after all, honey."
Home.
Fried onions, potatoes, meatloaf.
Grandma and Davy passing the ketchup.
My real mother,
the angry, suspicious one, asks:
"Why are you late?
What've you been up to now?"
Churning stomach,
I show her my purchase,
say quietly: "Nothing, Mother.
I just went to Womrath's.
And I bought a book."

DIVORCE

My father's sending us paperbacks now.
We already have *The Divided Family:
How Sometimes Divorce Is the Answer.*
Today's is *How to Mend What's Broken.*
I donate them to the library.
If he thinks reading

mass-market pop psychology
will help his case, he's a fool.
I've heard that divorce
is sweeping the nation.
Or at least the Bronx.

TURPENTINE

Frantic, Rachel calls from the school gym.
"Maisie, you have to get back here!
The murals are falling off the walls.
We need to get them back up."
I gallop over.
Rachel and I re-glue, tape,
sometimes hammer using small nails.
But Rachel's getting edgy.
I try to lighten things up,
take a large paintbrush and point it at her.
"This is a stickup.
Hands in the air, or else!"
"Maisie!
Can't you take anything seriously
besides yourself?"
Of course, that shuts me up.
Shuts me down.
True, the dance is tomorrow.
I look over at her determined face,
lips pursed, shoulders cramped.
"This means a lot to me, Maisie.
Everyone knows I'm in charge.
I have to be good at something, don't I?"
"I'm trying to help," I whisper.
She shrugs.

Maybe this is about Gino?
But I don't ask.

Once the murals are restored,
turpentine helps me clean up all the gunk.
I wish there was another kind of turpentine
you could use to remove
the neverland yearnings in your heart

LIKE A PINWHEEL

I have my outfit for the dance.
A shawl Kiki lent me à la Maria.
A flare felt skirt from last year.
And a peasant blouse from Grandma.
But as I'm putting myself together,
Judith plants herself in the middle of my room,
Medea to my Maria,
turning around in slow motion
like an off-duty pinwheel, staring,
her mouth a downturned, dark-maroon sliver.
"Look at this mess! You're a pig!"
Her accusations have no particular order:
"selfish, lousy, spoiled rotten . . ."
She's a walking thesaurus for hateful words.
Somewhere in the Bronx, there's
a mother telling her daughter,
"Wow! You look beautiful, darling.
Nobody can compare."
Judith's put-downs don't make me
want to straighten up my room.
"Can't you lay off me?

You never lay off me."
She growls, "Be careful, young lady,
or you're not going anywhere."
I send my grandmother
a mental message:
When will you tune in?!
This is my life.

GENERAL FUSSING

Must shower, dress, do hair,
general fussing.
I hear her footsteps.
The mother I want has a tray of food for me,
says, "I'm so proud of you!
Will you get someone to take pictures
of the gym for me?
Let's get you dressed, my pretty."
The mother I have says,
"You are *not* going to this dance
or anywhere else tonight!"
My life is one of those fairy tales
where the witch eats the child.
"And if you don't shape up,
you won't get to the Chardas next week, either."
That's our once-a-year family reunion party
at the famous Hungarian restaurant.
But I'm not thinking about that now!
When she leaves, I put on makeup,
the scoop-neck top, a tiny belt, and the flare skirt,
back-comb my hair over and over.
Nobody is there to say how adorable I look.
Which I do, minus
the smoldering red flame
under my eye.

MY REAL LIFE

Six thirty.
I sneak out through the kitchen
to the back stairs, burst out of my building
like a freedom fighter of my own personal
Hungarian Revolution.
I don't know where Richie is
or if he's coming.
He mentioned it once,
but then it never came up again.
Probably too many land mines at home.

In the streets, I overhear the happy rumble
of radios and televisions,
sniff the almost-done roasts,
face the evening's tired traffic,
and finally, nearing the gym,
step into a better life.

DEVIL IN THE MAKING

The dance floor vibrates:
music, lights, movement.
West Side Story means girls
in heavy makeup, kitten heels.
There are a hundred flirty Carol Lawrences.
The boys act Jets cool.
Rachel's wearing 100 percent black
to set off her bright-turquoise eye shadow.
Off-the-shoulder blouse, wide skirt.
She's a gorgeous Anita.
Richie O'Neill's already there,
with greaser hair like Bernardo.
He's no Ken Leroy.
Still, he's cuter than ever . . .
Oh! He's walking my way.
I hope he doesn't remember
I demanded that he kiss me.
Then demanded that he not.
But then Peter Collins from homeroom—
the movie star version—heads my way.
Richie cuts him off.
"Do you want to dance?"
Richie reaches for my hand.
There are so many boys here.
Greg Barkus, Ron Lopez look so cool!
I want to kiss all the Jets and the Sharks.
Well, maybe that's a bad idea,
so I say, "Sure, Richie."
He sings "Maria" into my ear.
I feel his hard body pushing against mine.
*"Maria, Maria, Maria . . .
say it soft and it's almost like praying."*

Richie's got a great voice!
I've never been this close to him.
The rest of the room fades.
It turns out my body is made of electricity!
I'm not sure when, who,
but someone switched it on.
"The most beautiful sound I ever heard ..."

PRETTY AND WITTY

Rachel lindies with Gino.
Out of the corner of my eye
I see how he moves! Wow!
There's a circle around them now.
Everyone's clapping.
It's like the Jets and the Sharks
are right here in our gym!
A tall, thick boy suddenly moves close
to Richie and me.
Not even skipping a beat,
Richie turns and
knocks into this kid hard.
This boy grunts meanly.
I recognize him, the jerk who felt me up!
Someone mentions his name:
Timmy O'Hara.
A scuffle.
Everyone leaves the dance floor
and freezes like you do
in a game of Spud
to watch Richie going at this boy hard.
First, a fist fight,
then Timmy tackles Richie

and they're both down on the floor.
Then back up again.
Richie's arms are like hammers,
his legs, too.
He's kicking, muttering curses.
Someone whispers, "That's karate!"
Timmy's trying to protect himself.
But Richie has him locked up.
Teachers zip over to them,
separate them, which isn't easy,
usher Richie and Timmy out of there.

Rachel, as dance chair,
feels she has to take charge,
so she chases them.
I should follow.
I should do something!
But Gino appears next to me,
stands so close,
his arm brushes mine.
We both say "wow" a few times.
But we drop using words.
Arms brushing arms.
I hardly breathe.
I can't speak.
Finally I get the courage
to actually look at him.
His hazel eyes are ponds of color.
His cheekbones look like geographical formations.
His mouth is moving,
but I can't take in actual words.
I just gaze at him.
"Yes," he says. "Yes,"

as if he was answering a question
he knew I was asking.

FOR ONCE

Richie's allowed back into the dance.
He's overheated, troubled.
I thank him for being a hero.
I want him to grab me and tell me
he'd do anything for me.
I want to feel my body turn on
like streetlights again.
"I don't want to become my father,"
he whispers nervously.
My sisterly feelings swoosh back.
Electricity is off.
"You're nothing like him, Richie!
You wanted to protect me."
I give him a chaste kiss on the cheek.
He turns his face toward me,
lips available.
I peck him quickly again,
not sure how to say what I feel.
Not sure what I feel.

LIFE HAPPENS HERE

It's still humid in the early May midnight.
Richie walks me home,
A new Bronx is revealed,
a tragic, beautiful Broadway theater set,
chain-link fencing, graffiti,
random sneakers and baseball hats
littered on the cement,
saying life happens here.
For once I do feel pretty and witty,
as if stage lights are on me.
All over again,
I want to dive into Richie's arms,
feel his face, his chest,
sense that he wants me,
must have me impossibly close.
Richie grabs me around the waist
and comes in for a kiss.
My lips part.

I smell mint on his breath.
I really can't stand the smell of mint.
Doesn't he know that?
He should know that.
"Not on the street." I pull back.

CRIME SCENE

When I open the front door to our apartment,
the living room is ominously ablaze,
like a crime scene.
"You better go," I say.
Richie stops, looks, blurts out:
"Oh! Okay." Then, "Bye,"
and with an impressive amount of speed,
takes his sexy *West Side Story* self
right out of our hallway.

TRIBUNAL

Inside, sitting in a genetic tribunal
are Judith, Grandma Ruth,
Great-Aunt Dalvinka.
Impartial glasses of sherry sit,
but from my family's faces
I see the verdict is in:
I'm already guilty.
They begin elucidating the list
of penances to come as if they'd rehearsed it.
Number one is that I'll be docked
from the annual Hungarian gathering
at the Chardas restaurant.
I growl, "Big deal!"
But as the only grandchild who's been invited,
they know how special it is to me.
"Unless you seriously shape up,
you'll miss it," says my grandmother.
"You know, Gran, I never could
count on you, anyway.

You're always busy! So busy!
I suppose you think I'm a terrible,
rotten kid, a devil in the making!"
"Maisie!" snorts my great-aunt Dalvinka.
"Do not speak that way to your grandma!"
I ignore her, continue,
"Maisie went out despite a messy room.
Thus, she must burn at the stake.
Got a match anyone? I'll light myself up!"
Turns out this is almost their exact plan.
I look at their waxy, moonlit faces.
Tonight, when my grandma should be asleep
tossing with old-lady insomnia,
she appears in our living room,
taking her daughter's side.
They're all useless!
Upshot: I'm not allowed to see
Rachel for a while.
As if *Rachel* were the problem!

DAVY

My brother is refusing to learn
a new piano piece.
Mother is insisting.
I've never heard him stand up to her like this.
She sits down next to him
and bangs out some chords.
"That's not the fingering," he says.
"You're cheating!"
If that was me talking,
there would be flesh on flesh.
But her voice just gets louder.

He smashes the keyboard.
She shouts something.
The piano lid snaps shut.
Davy passes my room to go to his.
"She's a bitch!" he mumbles,
as if making a fresh discovery.
I didn't even know he knew the word.
He slams his bedroom door.
What is going on with my brother?

MY OWN JAMES JOYCE

Housebound, no fleeing to Rachel's.
I comb our bookshelves,
discover a torn paperback volume of
A Portrait of the Artist as a Young Man
that Richie must have stuck in my school bag
and my mother put away.
I figure it will be way too hard
to understand.
But I start to read:
"Once upon a time
and a very good time it was
there was a moocow coming down
along the road . . ."
Somehow, this seems like
the most wonderful sentence to me.
Playful. Funny. Unexpected.
I love it!
Trapped in my room,
I'm meeting one of the great minds.
I'm getting hooked on *Portrait*!

CHARDAS NIGHT

I've been an angel
(if you consider that while angels did dishes
they also secretly sneered).
But I did hunker down, and now,
two weeks later,
I'm given a reprieve
to go to the Chardas.
I discovered the real reason she reversed her decision:
She paid the deposit months ago.
So what? I'm excited anyway.
Rachel has always asked to see
Hungarians at play in their natural habitat,
so she's coming.
"Hungarians at play?" I said. "Good luck!"
"Do you want to invite Gino?" I asked
before my brain could put the brakes on.
"It might be more fun for you."
"Thanks, Maisie! We won't eat a lot.
Anyway, he gave me a ring!"
A ring?!!
I didn't realize he'd go that far.
I tell myself this has nothing to do with me.
Still I'm shattered.

So Rachel, Gino, and I crowd in the back seat
of a taxi, driving to Manhattan.
Grandma, Mom
pinched together up front.
Great-Aunt Dalvinka has gone ahead since she lives nearby.
Grandma Ruth is wearing sparkly blue earrings.
Her eyes are outlined in black.
I tell her she looks like a teenager.

She says, "Truth is, I love compliments.
Hungarians are vain!"
Gino laughs.
Rachel is folded into him just like I would be
if I had any luck in love.

Finally, we pull up to a white building.
A man in a uniform trimmed in gold
valets our car.
Grandma, Mother,
Rachel, Gino, and I walk together
through the fancy carved doors
into a big hall with dim lights.
Someone dressed in a starched peasant shirt
plays the violin,
telling a story that's sweet—bittersweet.
Rache's face lights up.

CELEBRATE!

Delicious smells.
Goulash? Paprika? Onion?
People I don't remember
squish me in tight, perfumed hugs,
say, "Ooh, Maisie, you're getting to be
such a young lady!"
Great-Aunt Dalvinka appears.
She's put actual feathers in her hair
and trots around on high clickety shoes,
offers chewy kisses
from her wine-red lips,
whisks me onto the dance floor.
I guess all is forgiven.

Her mouth opens in a smile so wide,
I can see her gold teeth.
She hollers to Gino and Rachel:
"Shana madelas, come,
celebrate like Hungarians!"
So Rachel and Gino dance with us, too.
I am observing them
as if I were in science lab,
looking through a microscope.
Is he in love with her?
She adores him, that's for sure.
But sometimes I catch him
looking at me with such intensity!
I'm dreaming.
I must be dreaming.
Anyway, "He. Is. Off. Limits,"
I repeat to myself.
After a few glasses of wine,
I manage to forget about him.
We eat every kind of food,
starting with kohlrabi soup,
paprikash, palacsinta, and then, of course,
three kinds of strudel.
Mostly I watch everyone talk, drink, tell jokes,
until the music gets louder
and they crowd onto the dance floor,
kick their legs out.
"They're dancing the Chardas,"
I inform Rachel and Gino.
"Let's try it," says Gino.
I say, "It's not easy!
Unless you have springs in your thighs . . ."
But he grabs our hands,

and as we go down
in a deep plié, all three of us
fall over, hysterical.

A COUSIN OF HERSELF

Across the room my mother's laughing,
as if it's something she did all the time,
as if she always throws her head back
and stomps her foot
to release all the mirthful energy.
Grandma leads us over to her,
but I pull back.
"Come," she insists.
"*Don't!* She hates me."
But strangely, when I get close,
my mother kisses me on the cheek!
Then she kisses Rachel, too, even Gino,
probably because everyone can see us.
"She's like a cousin of herself,"
I whisper to them.

HOW LIFE WILL BE

Grandma dances without stopping.
We push ourselves through the crowd and join her;
the layers of my dress are flying.
People belt out Hungarian folk songs;
they're all emotional,
their features melting into gladness for once.
When it's over, I hug everyone good night,
gripping them so hard

I think, maybe, after this night,
this is how life will be:
My mother will laugh
and dance and be happy.
And so will I.

Great-Aunt Dalvinka stays to pay the bill.
Outside we wait to catch a cab.
Drowsy as we head uptown,
Rachel whispers,
"You always said your family was awful!
I think they're wonderful."
I try to explain:
"It was completely different tonight."
Rachel's eyelids are closed in girlfriend bliss.
She snuggles against Gino.
I catch his eyes in the back seat.
He winks at me.
A current passes through my body,
as if I've been mildly electrocuted.

RESPECT

The next day,
there's another letter from my father.
Dear Maisie,
I heard about the party,
I even drove by the Chardas.
I wanted to see you,
but I left.
I didn't want to make a scene.
Look, as your father,
respect is due to me.

But you're acting as if I'm some kid
from school you want to punish,
not your FATHER!
I've written almost every day,
pleading, explaining, apologizing.
But you ignore me.
I left badly, but it would have hurt
no matter what.
Maisie, you have to understand,
and Davy as well.
I miss you.
But I won't cry over you.

ANOTHER DANCE

What does he mean,
he won't cry?
Crying's the least he could do.
Then I wonder, can he do anything
to change my mind about him?
There is, but I can't bear to think about it.
So I tear up his dumb, idiotic note,
walk to my window, and toss it out.

Pieces flutter down into the courtyard
where I spot two men doing a strange dance.
It's Richie! And Mr. O'Neill!
They're kicking, lunging, doing karate.
It's almost artistic, but masculine,
powerful: kick, lunge, chop, chop.
This must be how his dad was
before Vietnam.

AIN'T FAIR

Richie calls later.
I start to say how happy I am
that he and his dad are getting along.
"It didn't last.
I should have known 'karate dad'
was too good to be true.
When we got upstairs,
he started in on Regina.
I called the police.
He swore he'd kill me.
Naturally, with all the fuss,
I haven't done my French homework.
Moreau will fail me.
Ce n'est pas juste."
"Huh?"
"'*Pas juste* means 'it ain't fair'!"
"*Isn't* fair," I correct him.
"Ain't," he repeats.
"Sometimes *ain't* is the right word, Maisie."
"You have a point, Richie.
It ain't fair."

LOSING PATIENCE

The next day,
a car trails behind me, honking.
So annoying. Who even does that?
Honk. Honk.
Then I look.
No! *NO!*
It's my father's Caddy!
I start walking fast, running.
What's he doing here?
Louder sustained blasts.
"C'mon, Maisie."
He's leaning out the window.
"Stop! Talk to me! I insist!"
I speed up, frantic to escape.
He parks, slams the door,
runs to catch up to me.
"Go away!" I holler.
"Go away! I hate you."
"Maisie, you will stop.
And you will talk to me.
If you want to scream at me,
scream at me,
but you mustn't run away.
I'm your father!"
"Father? What father?"

BIG PHONY

He's faking that he's out of breath.
That's just like him, the big phony.
"What? What do you want, Joe?"
"You don't call me 'Joe'!
You call me 'Dad'!"
"I don't have anyone
I want to call 'Dad'!
Not anymore!"
"You're breaking my heart, kid."
"Poor Daddy has a broken heart!
Let's all feel sorry for you.
Lest we forget who the only important person
on the planet has always been!"
"I don't blame you for being angry."
His voice cracks.
"It was wrong to disappear
in the middle of the night.
But I swear to you, I'll never . . ."
There's water sliding down his cheek.
He's weeping.
It's loud, too.
Maybe the word is *sobbing*.
Embarrassed, I turn,
open the passenger door,
and get into his Caddy.
I don't want to be part of the mayhem,
the turmoil, of this street
in this mad city.

BE REASONABLE

He's jumped back into the driver's seat.
"I've been writing, calling,
sending flowers every week."
"Never got any dopey flowers."
"Your mother didn't . . . ?
Well, I shouldn't be surprised,"
he mumbles.
Flowers? Is he kidding?
Like flowers would have made a difference!
"What are you doing here, anyway?
Is it because you want me
to come and live with you now?
When?" I prod. "And what about Davy?"
He says, "Wait a minute, Maisie, hold on . . .
Be reasonable."
My hand reaches for the door handle.
"Why am I the one who has to be reasonable?
I'm the kid!"
"You're some character," he says.
"I don't want to be a character,
I want to be someone's daughter!"
I go to open the passenger door.
But he hits the lock,
turns the engine on, pulls out.
I'm stuck now.

We drive for a while, silently.
Well, I'm silent.
He's saying greasy, meaningless words.
I've got the "you're not wanted"
  stone lodged in my chest.

WORD VACATION

"Look," he says, "it's not that simple."
He starts talking about
his so-called girlfriend.
"I already know about your tramp.
She's more important to you
than your own goddamn children!"
He stops the car.
His face drops into his hands.
My adulterous father is undone.
"Don't ask me to feel sorry for you, Dad.
You're a *jerk*!"
I don't want to hear his answer,
so I turn on his radio.
It's on WEVD, a Spanish station.
My dad doesn't speak Spanish.
Neither do I.
I recognize the words "*mi corazón*"
because WEVD is the same station
I listen to in my room!
I don't tell him that.
"Why do you listen to music
that you don't understand?"
"That's exactly the point," he says.
"I like not understanding.
It's a word vacation."

MI CORAZÓN

If I weren't sitting
in his double-crossing black Caddy,
I would've never known
that both of us need a vacation
from words we do understand.
Mi corazón; mi duele el corazón.
For a minute I'm his girl again.
But that one thing we share isn't enough.
"You forgot me once. Forget me again!
You don't have a daughter anymore."
Then I'm unlocking and exiting his car,
right into a puddle, gunk on my shoes,
lost in the treacherous, muddy gray-brown streets
of the endless Bronx.

GO FLY A KITE

Judith almost trips me
when I finally walk into the apartment.
"Well!" she says, hunched shoulders,
narrowed eyes. "You're a little sneak!
Davy saw you get into the Caddy.
So now you're talking
to the cheating bastard!"
"But Davy didn't hear what I said.
I told Dad to go fly a kite!"
She glowers.
"Why should I believe you?"
"Because I'm telling the truth, Mother!"
"You were always his favorite,"
she says. "Always will be."
"Yeah, well he left me behind, didn't he?"
"I said 'his favorite.'
That doesn't mean he loved you.
Who could love you?"
She grips her hands on my shoulders,
shakes me,
until I think my head will tumble off,
roll on the ground, and crash.
"You have no idea
how much I hate him," I scream.
"Even more than I hate you!
I'd rather be dead
than ever talk to him again."
I pry off her hands, run to my room,
barricade the door.
Then I go into my closet
and sit on top of my shoes,

biting my lip, refusing the tears
that rub against my eyelids.

A BRAT VACATION

"What am I supposed to do with you?"
she says that night.
"You should send me away, Mom."
"Believe me, I wish I could!"
"You mean to a leper colony?"
"Do you know of a leper colony?"
she asks.
"I can try to find out."
"Shut up, Maisie!"
"Or I could go with Rachel.
True, she isn't going to a leper colony,
but she is going to summer camp.
Starts in three weeks."
"You don't deserve summer camp!"
she huffs.
"But you deserve to have me gone.
And maybe I could learn
to be a better person," I say.
"Just think: Summer days without me.
A brat vacation."
"A brat vacation . . . ?"
She turns the words around
like a caramel-filled hard candy.
"Hmmmm . . .
I'll get your cheating father to pay."

AWAY FROM HER

Rachel isn't home.
I have to tell someone my news.
Summer camp! Escape!
Four weeks away from her!
I look out the window
but see no sign of Richie.
Come to think of it,
I haven't seen him for days.
So I dial his number.
"Hey," I say cheerfully.
"Hey," he answers.
I almost don't recognize his voice.
Low. Like he's a melancholic tuba.
"You okay?"
"*Ça dépend*," he says.
"Please. English, Richie!" I insist.
"Depends on what?"
"My mom left," he confesses.
"It got too much for her.
Dad's going nuts."
"God, I'm so sorry.
Why do parents leave kids with people
they themselves can't handle?"

There's no point in telling him about camp now.
My voice drops, too.
Like the other tuba in the heartbroken band.

LIKE EVERYONE ELSE'S MOTHER

Voilà!
At the end of June.
Judith drives Rachel and me
to Grand Central Terminal
to meet the counselors and kids.
She's fiddling with my hair,
telling me to have a good summer,
checking my suitcase,
asking what she needs to send me,
acting like everyone else's mother.
For once.
As if she'd been admitted
to the brain transfusion unit
and they gave her a new one,
plus, no charge, a new heart.

GOODBYE

Time to go; we pile into the train.
It pulls out of the station.
Rachel and I are waving.
All the kids are.
I'm waving a lot! Goodbye, witch!
You can't hurt me now!
Then I spot Judith's face in the crowd.
I have to look again.
Her head is bobbing.
She's bawling!
Bawling into her handkerchief
as if she's lost a puppy dog.
Maybe, seeing me leave,
she imagines she loves me.

WHO I AM

Rachel tells me Gino practically begged her
to spend the summer in the city.
"I nearly gave in." She sighs.
"But I decided to let him really miss me.
I've made it too easy for him."
"What do you mean, too easy?" I prod.
"Some things have to be sacred
between a man and a woman." She sighs.
"Of course!" I nod understandingly,
trying not to roll my eyes, add,
"I guess both your hearts will break a little."
"Don't pretend to know what I feel,"
says Rachel.
She gets this way about Gino.
"Of course not!"
Later on she says,
"Sorry if I sounded unpleasant.
It's just difficult to be without him."
I make understanding clucking noises.
"We didn't go all the way, Maisie. Yet.
But he's so sexy."
I only say "uh-huh" in a distracted way,
as if Gino's sexiness
is the last thing on my mind.

The train sways on a turn,
then rebalances and picks up speed.
"Okay," says a calmer Rachel,
"you should know there's an award called
'Girl of the Week.'
Even if you turn your nose up at it,

you secretly want to win it,
get a pink patch that says
'Color War Special Citation.'
You should try, Maisie!
You can prove to your mother
that you're nothing like her."
"You mean that not every atom in my body
is horrendously destructive?"
By the time we pull into the small country train station,
we've both cooled down.
Rachel says:
"I do love you, Maisie.
At least most of the time."

First game, I single-handedly
score more points in basketball
than the entire blue team,
which makes me a local hero.
That night I write Richie to tell him,
but mostly I'm worried.
He's home without his mother,
only his younger sister and freaky, infuriated father.

WHAT I'M NOT GOOD AT

I'm good at basketball.
What I'm *not* good at:
    1) keeping my mouth shut to other campers
    2) keeping my mouth shut in general
    3) hospital corners
    4) neatness
    5) ceasing and desisting drawing
unflattering, hideous pictures of people
Mostly I talk back to my counselor.
She says I have anger problems.
I say, "You would, too, if . . ."
"If *what*?" she asks.
"Do you want to share anything with me?
I'm a good listener."
"No," I say in bad tones.
I can't stop myself.
Even though Judith is far away
and can't pick on me,
can't reach out and smack me,
I hear her bloody voice
tearing me down,
feel her as distinctly
as if she were bunking
right next to me.

ANGER PROBLEMS

The next day I've scored the most points
in Color War games in the history of the camp.
So when Girl of the Week is announced,
I dare think, it will be me!

But no, it's Pam.
The following week it's Rachel.
I grit my teeth.
I don't like having anger problems.
But what do you do if you are angry?

GIRL OF THE WEEK

I decide to make an effort.
Am polite, helpful.
I spike the ball in volleyball
so we kill the other side.
My counselor says, "That is a good use
for your pent-up emotions."
So now I love her for being just plain nice.

OUT LOUD

On Friday the last medal of the summer is awarded.
Missy Henkins, a tiny, useless
but neat troglodyte
who's never scored a single point
for her team, gets it!
Unfortunately, because I have anger issues,
I say this out loud.
"Oh, Maisie!" Rachel sighs.
"You're supposed to be on my side,"
I say.
"I wish you didn't make it
so difficult sometimes," she says.
Then she gets busy writing Gino
for about a thousand hours.

TROUBLEMAKERS

That night, after curfew,
I put new batteries in my flashlight,
wake up Rachel to convince her
to go down to the dock,
which we've discussed once or twice.
"Let's sneak into the nudist camp!"
We've all heard the Misirlou being played daily,
echoing across the water
like a sweet invitation
to another universe.
Rachel says, "You must be crazy!
I'm not here to cause trouble.
I'm here to make sure Gino thinks about me
day and night."

MISIRLOU

The moonlight is bright.
I paddle to the distant side of the bank,
right up to their dock,
fasten the canoe and climb up the stairs,
head toward the lights of the campus.
As I get closer, I hear the familiar chords
of the mesmerizing song.
And then I'm nearing a dance floor
right out in the open.
Turns out the people are not completely naked,
but they're not exactly wearing that much, either.
There are legs, arms, chests, midriffs,
and bellies on display.
A few people spot me.
Their eyes widen in surprise.

I'm the youngest person I see.
Everyone is friendly.
I tell them I need a break from sports camp,
which seems to make sense to them.
Right off, I ask them to teach me the Misirlou.
You wave your arms and put one foot
in front of the other
but quickly retract it,
then you turn and place your arms
on the next person's shoulder
so everyone is dancing in unison.
It's not that difficult.
I love the music. The singer's voice wavers;
there's longing in it,
but her longing is beautiful.

A MILLION KISSES

After a while, the sky begins to lighten;
it's getting to be morning.
They give me a million kisses.
They keep saying I'm a great dancer.
Tears of gratitude drip onto my tanned arms
as I row back to camp
on the perfectly still waters of the lake.
I tie up the canoe, lope up the hill,
and sneak back into our bunk.
I no longer care about Girl of the Week.
This is good, because, let's face it,
when you have anger issues
you aren't likely to get awards;
you're likely to get thrown out of camp.

Which is exactly what happens to me.

NICE TO YOU

So you are sent home on the very same train
that left Grand Central
three weeks ago.
You look out the window,
watch the scenery roll by in reverse.
You arrive home worried, decide to avoid
your hissing mother.
You tear up the pathetic letters
that keep coming from your father,
reeking of men's scented shaving cologne
and suntan lotion.
You wish you could believe anything he says.

You go to your bedroom window,
looking for a sign of Richie.
He doesn't show.
You lie in bed,
hope you'll meet more people
who dance the Misirlou,
who can be nice to you,
so incredibly nice
that if you feel all bottled up and lonely,
you'll be able to melt
in a soft, sweet way again.

KNOCKING, KNOCKING

I knock on Richie's door.
Nobody answers.
Three days in a row.
Nothing.
I leave a note for him.
Dear James Joyce,
I write,
I'm your biggest fan.

TOO MUCH VALKING

Then one humid morning,
temperature above 90 degrees,
I stop by my grandmother's to bring her cookies
Davy and I made.
"Oy, these feet! I vas stomping around
Manhattan yesterday," she says.
"Too much valking."
She won't say why she went, though
I know exactly why.
She was with Judith talking to
a Madison Avenue divorce lawyer.
My mother scribbled a name down
on her phone pad.
Leibovitz, Elkins and Schwartz.
I don't ask Grandma to corroborate.
I let her make me tea
and serve our lumpy sweets.
Sometimes, wordlessly, Davy and I
will take out flour, butter, eggs
and concoct something to soothe us.

Grandma tells me Davy's music teacher
thinks he's special.
Then she pauses.
"I worry about that boy, you know?"
I'm silent. I didn't know.
I don't tell her that maybe Davy is different.
But he's still Davy.
And if he loves a boy, he loves a boy.
Like Pavel, a genius. Like Thomas Eakins.
Bernstein. Frances Bacon.

But I don't dare give her any information
that could get back to Judith.

RANDOM AND ORGANIZED

"Personally, I don't care that you've been
kicked out of camp!"
Kiki says when I drop by her studio.
"Camp's so conventional, so bourgeois!"
Being bourgeois is a sin to Kiki.
"That's why I'm so glad
you're going to learn a language,"
she says. "Expose yourself to another culture,
you will widen your world."

I think, in the back of my mind,
that I'll have Mrs. Moreau for French.
She's undoubtedly as horrible as everyone says.
Richie can't stand her tight, bony face
that makes it clear
we're all *sans espoir,*
désespéré;

hopeless.
Kiki's studio's the only place I want to be now.
That's where my *espoir* still lives.
Kiki says she's happy I visit.
She gives me oil Cray-Pas to sketch with, says,
"This is the good place I come to screw my head on right,"
and "Your oil technique is getting better!"
Even though my designs are abstract,
they have a certain form to them,
both random and organized.
I'm inspired by Jackson Pollock.
Kiki showed me a book about him.
At first I didn't get it.
But then I looked at his imitators.
You can tell how good he is
when you realize that under the chaos of color,
there's a logic and a freedom,
not that I paint anything like him.
Pollock's in a class of his own.
I wonder if he ever went to summer camp
and caused a damn ruckus.
I bet he did.

POLLOCK

It turns out that Kiki and Jackson
were good buddies at the Cedar Tavern
in Greenwich Village.
He drank to excess and died at age forty-four
in a car accident.
Kiki's face lights up with reverence
when she talks about him.
I'd love to ask her if *she* ever thought
about quitting drinking.
But I don't.

Kiki says she's rapturous every time
she comes home from spending the afternoon
at the Guggenheim Museum
on upper Fifth Avenue.
Which she does after her classes some days.
"What a structure. It's a spiral!
Inside you feel grand and liberated somehow.
It helps you see the art.
It's brilliant, Maisie."
She admits she cried for hours when
Frank Lloyd Wright, the architect
who designed the museum,
died before it even opened.
When she needs to calm herself down,
as she told me,
"I have to remind myself that Wright,
this genius,
was anti-Semitic.
Then I get a grip."
I've found a world, a complicated, vast world,

that leaves this Bronx borough behind.
A world I somehow belong to.

NEGATIVE SPACE

Kiki carefully considers my drawings
and says my work has "authority"
and that not everyone can use space like I do.
"If only you were living in Manhattan!
The High School of Art and Design
would be the place for you."

One day she surprises me.
She makes a frame with a mat
for one of my small watercolors.
Beautiful! Perfect.
Once I gave my mother an ebony pencil sketch
of a head, three-quarter view
with chiaroscuro shading.
I worked on it for hours.
It lay around our house until one day
Judith took it to a professional.
But even after I specifically explained
to her how important negative space was,
how it sets off the drawing,
makes your eye focus,
it was cropped, imprisoned,
without any white space to set it off.
It was cramped and ugly.
Ruined.

WHAT'S IN HERE

"You know, I don't invite just anyone here,"
Kiki says in her somber, soft voice.
She hands me a small canvas and a palette,
points to the tubes of oils
on a table between us.
"Where do I begin?" I ask.
"That's between you and the canvas,"
says Kiki, lighting up again.
"Personally, I start with what's in here."
She points to her gut
and then her heart.
Then she points to her private place.
I gasp.
"Don't be such a prude,"
she chortles, knows she got me,
takes a brush and loads it with grays and blues,
makes a slash clear across her canvas
as if she's slicing someone in half.
"Are you angry?" I ask.
"Shhh," she says kindly.
"I don't like to talk in here.
This is the place
where I don't have to take care of anyone,
be anything, say anything.
It frees me up and gives me a time to . . ."
"To what?"
I ask when she pauses.
"Let's just paint, Maisie, shall we?"

TALENT IS THE FLIP SIDE OF A CURSE

I wouldn't have thought Kiki—
who's mostly a big yapper—
could actually *be* quiet.
She puts on a Billie Holiday album.
I mix some colors, add a little black
and some linseed oil, the way
Kiki taught me.
I close my eyes, think of my art heroes,
Jackson Pollock, Pavel Tchelitchew, George Grosz;
what would they do now?
I bring my brush close to the canvas.
It freezes midair.
"Just begin," Kiki whispers,
tosses her cigarette into an ashtray,
stabs it out.
"We paint because we *have* to.
I believe talent is the flip side of a curse."
Talent. That's what Richie said.
I force myself to make a line,
dividing the space in two.
I love how it looks on the white canvas,
so self-assured, so bold,
so not like me.

I make a few more strokes.
Pavel was born in Russia,
but he lived all over Europe,
spent his life loving a man, not a woman.
I wonder if I should tell Davy.

NOT THAT BLUE

As always, sooner or later,
I feel an engine turning on.
I mix colors and paint blotches of them,
wherever I want.
One color demands another; orange insists, "Blue!
You *have* to put blue next to me!"
I do, but I hear, "No, not *that* blue,
a *deeper* blue!"
Winsor & Newton paints have opinions!
"I'm too bright!" screams orange.
"I'm dominating the picture!
Soften me, dilute me with Cadmium Yellow Light!"
Or Alizarin Crimson will cry:
"I need Burnt Sienna, *now*!"
These colors are bossy!
Soon there is no white space left.
My canvas looks as if
there never *was* any white.
I even forget that Kiki's about four feet away from me.
I no longer detect her smoke
or the stale coffee on her table.
I'm not sure what this painting could be.
Yet.

TRAVEL BACK

It's dark outside.
Kiki taps me lightly, says,
"We should call it a day."
She walks over to my work,
turns to me, and stares, sizing me up.
"Are you ready to be on this journey?"
she asks.
My blank stare must tell her
I'm not following her.
"To be an artist.
You know, that's what you are, Maisie.
All of that confusion and hurt,
plus your soul, plus the lens you see through,
plus your natural ability to handle color,
line, and space makes you an artist.
In case you weren't sure, I'm telling you this.
You can hold on to that
when the quicksand comes.
There's always quicksand for us.
That's part of mastering anything."

I'm stunned.
I repeat her words to myself,
but I can't speak.
So I help her clean up
and walk to her building, into the kitchen.
She makes tea.
It takes a while for me to remember to use words,
as if I've traveled across the tundra of my brain,
and now I have to travel back again.
I will visit her words again and again.
"I'm an artist."

And: "*quicksand.*"
And: "hold on."

THE OUTLET

The front door swings open.
Rachel appears in her camp gear explaining
that her dad, Ken, is parking.
He picked her up a few days early.
She whispers to me,
"I couldn't stay away from Gino."
Then she sees how messy I am.
"Why are you covered in paint, Maisie?
And why are you here at *all*?"
"She's got the art bug all right,"
says Kiki, hugging her.
"So glad you're home, Rache."
"You mean she has the art bug, not like me, Mom?"
Rachel pulls away and asks me petulantly:
"Maisie," she asks,
"do you really like it that much?
Or are you just wanting
to hang around my mother?"
"I do—like it," I admit weakly (love it).
Rachel rolls her eyes, leads me into her room,
closes the door.
"Honestly, you do not want to be anything like Kiki,
I promise you.
She's a total mess of a human being.
And why would anyone
want to see her as a therapist?
She's just an old drunk."
"That's so mean, Rachel!"

"The truth is cruel sometimes," she says.
"You think my family is perfect,
but you're so wrong, Maisie.
I think your family is great,
you should appreciate them!
Here, there are bottles of liquor lying around.
You can hardly sit down
without finding one.
Kiki has wild mood swings.
She's clearly damaged in some profound way.
I always have to be
the calm, cool, and collected one,
especially for my brothers.
I'm the one everyone calls
for whatever mayhem is at hand;
I'm the disaster-free person."
She kicks off her sneakers
and throws them across the room.
"But one day, you'll see that
we quiet, responsible ones
can be hellions, too."
Her face is too red.
Does Rachel mean one day
she'll give *me* mayhem?

"Rache, honey." Kiki comes in.
"Tomorrow I bet President Kennedy
would give you the afternoon off
if you wanted to come into the studio
with me and Maisie."
"Maisie stinks of linseed oil,"
Rachel complains.
"And I want to go to Fordham Road.

Clean up, Maisie!
Boys don't like eau de turpentine."

FORDHAM ROAD

I wash like crazy,
but I still have oil paint all over me.
Prussian Blue on my fingertips,
Cadmium Red crusted on my arms.
I feel as if it is traveling through my veins, too.
When Rache and I walk down Fordham Road
it's too quiet between us.
"Don't be mad, Rache.
Being lost in making something
brings me back to myself.
I need an outlet."
"I thought *I* was your outlet."
"You're my best friend," I say.
"Are you sure? Maybe it's Kiki?"
"Are you kidding? Of course I'm sure!"
I hook her arm in mine.
I want Rache to feel safe,
so I say, "Your mom's great
but a little wacky, right?"
"She's the original wack job,"
Rache says, and grips my arm tightly.
"Well, promise not to tell Kiki
I called her 'wacky'!"
Rachel promises, but she will tell.
I don't blame her.
I wouldn't like it, either, if my mother
half fell in love with my best friend.

ANOTHER PLANET

But it's only when I'm at Rachel's
that I finally feel as if my skin
is like other people's skin,
not covering some alien form from another planet
out in a distant, silent universe
that nobody knows or cares about and never will.

WEDDING ANNIVERSARY

Nobody we know is around,
so we return to her apartment.
Rachel disappears to call Gino.
They talk for a decade at least.

Meanwhile, Kiki's planning a party
to celebrate her twenty-fifth wedding anniversary.
Kiki says, "You should come, Maisie,
you could meet other artists.
You'll fit right in."
I don't think she was only being nice;
Kiki really does think of me as an *artist*!
So I say, "You bet! I'll be there!"
Too much is happening too fast,
at least according to my stomach.

GRANDMA'S PHONE CALL

Grandma calls in the morning.
"Vhat cruel luck, Maisie!
It's your mom's birthday next veek.

It falls on the two-month anniversary
of his leaving.
Shall ve do something for her, shana?"
I don't say: What my mother needs,
I can't give her.
Won't give her.
And she doesn't want it, anyway.
"I'm stuck," my grandmother presses.
"Vhat to do?"
"I wish I knew, Grandma."
She sighs. "Maisie, maybe—
you and your mom could stop being enemies?"

That night I ask my mother, "Can we be friends?"
She snorts, "When monkeys fly."
I think, well, that's honest.

LEAKY BOAT

Still, even though she deserved to be left,
and Davy and I did not,
now we're all in the same leaky boat.
Judith's broken. Her hands shake.
She stays in her bedroom, shades drawn,
spends half the day on the phone
with her lawyer, Bill Liebowitz.
Sometimes I hear her tell Grandma
that Bill's going to make my father
pay big-time alimony.
But I believe she believes
that Bill will somehow get Joe
to come home.

BIRTHDAY CAKE

I knock on Davy's door.
He hides a magazine and seems sullen.
"Do you hate me, Davy?"
"No," he says.
"No?"
"No!"
"How was it while I was at camp?"
"She's getting worse," he mumbles.
"Did she hit you, Davy?"
"She wished she could.
But I would have clocked her," he says.
And he smiles,
as if the idea is suddenly very pleasing.

Finally, when I look across to Richie's apartment,
I see lights on.
After dinner, I tap on his door, explain:
"Judith's turning forty-one.
She is my mother . . ."
Richie doesn't quote James Joyce.
He tells me to bake a cake.
Literally, "Bake a cake!"
"You're so definite!"
"How can you go wrong with a cake?"
he asks.
So I decide for her worst birthday ever,
before I give up
to make a real effort—
it can't be that hard.
Anyway, Davy and I are baking buddies.

***

Richie, scrubbed and shiny
like a semiprecious stone,
brings flowers for her.
He's wearing a bright-blue shirt.
The plan is that Grandma will take
Judith out for dinner.
Meanwhile, Davy and I turn on the oven,
get out the flour, eggs, butter, mixing bowls, and
measuring cups, and get started.
Richie greases the pan.
The recipe calls for orange zest.
We're out of oranges
so we use lemon zest,
add more honey.
We get the batter to a good consistency.
Davy sets the timer.
We slip it in.

WHICH WAY WILL THIS GO?

It's late, late enough to watch Milton Berle
on *The Tonight Show*.
Davy is young enough to think
Uncle Milty is hilarious.
Richie puts his arm around me.
It rests on my shoulder.
Davy groans.
"Not here, Richie," I whisper.
Milty gets pie in his face.
It's always funny somehow.
Richie and Davy both go off the deep end laughing.
They take one look at me—

my face is stone—
and that cracks them up even more.
Seeing Richie laugh, though, is catching.
So now it's Richie and me
having the hilarities.
We can't stop even after Davy
recovers and changes the channel.
The oven timer finally goes off.
I remove the baking pan
and inhale the buttery aroma,
place it on top of the stove.
When I hear the front door buzz,
I gasp for air.
Which way will this go?

"Hi, Mrs. Meyers," says Richie
as she walks into the kitchen.
"Grandma was tired and went home,"
Judith explains, and just stands there
as if she doesn't comprehend English.
"This was Maisie's idea,"
says Richie proudly.
"It was supposed to have orange flavor,"
Davy adds,
"but we only had lemons."
Finally her eyes settle on our masterpiece.
Then, in front of our eyes,
the center of the cake
begins to crack, shrivel, and sink,
as if gravity itself
suddenly turned against us.
Now Mother is sinking, too,
down into a chair, her body dense,

as if she's going to fall
right through the kitchen floor,
descend into the core of the earth.

A SIMPLE CAKE

"You baked for me?"
she asks in a tremulous voice,
a voice I've never heard before.
Her face looks like one of those
cardboard puzzles
with some of the pieces missing.
"It looks awful now," Davy reports.
"I must have forgotten an ingredient,"
I explain miserably,
wait for her to say how,
naturally, I can't even manage
to make a simple cake.
"We followed the recipe,"
says Richie.
"Maisie tried real hard."

THIS MOMENT

She's silent. We all are.
The four of us just stare
at the disaster in front of us.
Finally, my mother whispers,
"It's fine, it's nice. Thank you."
Then her arms shoot out
and grab me by the waist.
She pulls me close, then Davy.

She grips us both to her.
Her head bobs on my shoulder.
Then I realize
the ungodly sound I hear is *her*,
whimpering, squeaking,
choking on the words *love you*.
Maisie, I think to myself, *remember* this moment!
The moment you've waited for.

YOU MARRIED HIM

Richie cuts us all slices.
My mother eats hers in silence.
Later she looks out the window
as if there's something
new to see in the ragged Bronx skyline.
Hope is a fiend, so I blurt,
"Mom, did you and Dad ever love each other?
Because you married him.
You had *us*."

BEAUTIFUL TOGETHER

She takes a long breath,
eats the last bit of cake, shrugs.
"There's one memory of the bastard,
well, before he was a bastard,
excuse my French, kids.
It was March,
we were on the Grand Concourse.
It was uncharacteristically warm
and I'd broken up with Stan.

I wasn't really over him.
Your dad and I were dating
but I was still a mess.

Joe found a spot under a large tree.
He was wearing a handsome tweed suit.
His green eyes seemed to be grinning.
I'd come from work.
I had on the loveliest lace blouse,
expensive shoes from a photo shoot.
Very flattering.
I think, if someone saw us,
they would have thought:
'Those two are beautiful together.'

DENTS

We dusted off a bench.
Then your dad asked me plain,
no joking around—
which was the exception, for him,
always the tease—to give him my hand.
He got flustered, began to propose.
'Haven't you noticed?' I interrupted.
'Noticed what?' he asked.
'My left eye has no vision, Joe.
I'm deformed.
There was an accident when I was five.'
'We all have dents,' he said,
then sat there calmly and quietly.
I fought back tears.
So then I said 'yes.'"
She glances at us, pauses.

"Don't get all misty-eyed, kids.
As you know, mainly he's a jerk."

DRESSY ENOUGH

The short peace between my mother and me
doesn't last.
Tonight I dress up for the party at Rachel's.
I don't invite Richie.
I could.
But I don't.
What does that make me?
The old Judith reappears, says:
"You're not going *anywhere*!
You're staying home to watch Davy."
"But, Mom, *you're* here!
We both don't need to be here!"
She starts screaming.
That's when I blurt out:
"Kiki says the problem in our house
is you!
She says you're crazy!"

I sprint past Judith
and run all the way to Rachel's.
Flowers everywhere! Balloons!
Something wonderful is cooking.
So festive!
But in her room, my friend is still in cutoffs!
True, she's a knockout without trying.
"When are you going to change
for the party, Rache?"
"I hate these evenings," she murmurs.

"Everyone smokes and smells of liquor.
It's gross."
Finally she does change
into a filmy, pale-blue blouse and jeans.
She looks like a cover girl,
but I wonder out loud,
"Is that really dressy enough?"

GENIUS PAINTERS

"Gino and I are going to the movies,"
she says, grins:
"I have him where I want him."
"Why didn't you tell me you wouldn't be here?"
"I would have if you weren't so busy
becoming a genius painter with my mother."
"Hold on there, tiger," I say.
"You know it's true, Maisie."
"Hey, no worries. I'll go home. Honestly."
"Don't be a fool," she says.
"You're just looking for love
in all the wrong places.
Anyway, before you know it,
my fabulous parents will get drunk.
You'll be bored."

PHONIES

"I don't want you to be upset with me, Rache."
She laughs. "I'm just giving you a hard time.
Don't be so serious.
Have a good time with the phonies!"

She hugs me, leaves in a perfume haze.
I dust the slightest bit of her rosy blush
on my cheeks.
I wonder if I'm pretty, too.
I give myself a kiss in the mirror.
I wish a boy were kissing me back.
But which boy?

FABULOUS GROWN-UPS

At about nine o'clock,
Kiki's living room
is officially packed and noisy.
Cigarette smoke diffuses faces,
makes me cough.
Kiki introduces me to everyone;
not only tells them I'm a painter
but brings out the drawing I gave her,
the one she had framed.
One woman studies it.
It's her friend Nastasia,
whose well-known gallery
in Manhattan
has sold her clients'
work to the Museum of Modern Art!
Nastasia looks right at me and smiles.
Kiki and Nastasia begin to argue.
Should I go to art school
or should I stay *away* from art school?
On the one hand,
I wish the floor would open up;
on the other, I wish I could record this
so my mother could see

these fabulous grown-ups
discussing my future.
As if it were an important topic!

LATER

I'm almost hyperventilating,
but the two of them
are still so intensely debating the pros and cons
of academia,
they forget I'm there!
I realize I'm in the middle
of some ancient power struggle.
I decide to lie low
and maybe later try to talk
to each of them one-on-one.
But soon Kiki and Nastasia
have wandered over to the piano
and they're harmonizing
with a folk singer they both know.
They're drinking and laughing at stuff
I don't understand.

EXTRA WHEEL

It dawns on me:
I don't belong with Kiki's friends;
I belong with Rachel.
But now Gino is head over heels for her.
And I'm the extra wheel.
I need to say to Rachel,
"I'm so grateful you're my friend

and that you took me into your family.
That's so generous.
I'm so lucky your mother took pity on me.
But *you* are the most important person
in my life, Rachel. Not Kiki.
You have to believe me."
But I don't say it.
I'm not sure it's the truth.

THE BIG THINGS

Home. I read *A Portrait of the Artist*
until midnight.
Judith's still sitting at her sewing machine,
under a lamp with a dull bulb.
She's going to ruin her good eye.
I don't interrupt her, though.
I suppose she's waiting until morning
to punish me for leaving.
I want to ask her about her lawyer, Liebowitz.
But anything I might say
brings me into the red zone of danger.
Instead, I take the long phone cord
and tiptoe into my room to call Rache.
She must be home by now.
I want to hear about her date.

GINO

"The last three weeks,
Gino missed me so much.
He couldn't keep his hands off me!

I can't keep him under control forever,"
she says conspiratorially,
as if I have my very own
Gino's-hands-all-over-me problem.
I think she wants me to say,
"Well then, just do it."
But I refuse to say that.
So I ask what they talk about.
"He loves Kennedy as much as I do.
And Pete Seeger and this folk singer Joan Baez.
I just love how he thinks.
In an abstract way," she says,
"but not like most artists
who may think they're abstract
but mainly are involved only
with themselves
and the minutiae of their petty lives.
I'm so sick of *artistes*."
"Are you talking about me, Rachel?"
"That's a perfect example
of being self-centered, Maisie,"
she says.
"Gino ponders the big things.
He recites passages from *The Prophet*
and plays a funky harmonica.
What I mostly like is that
this boy finds me exotic.
That's the exact word he used.
Exotic! *Moi!*
I catch him staring at me
at the oddest moments,
as if I were a foreign substance,
like I am an equation

and he wants to figure it out
if I can give him a little more time.
Well, there *is* a formula.
He just has to put me first!
Everyone else can get lost!"
"Is that 'everyone else' me, Rachel?"
"Jeez, Maisie, do you realize
how self-absorbed you sound?"

UH-OH!

I'm remembering how, a few months ago,
Rachel said:
"Teach me how to flirt; I'll pay you."
I guess it worked,
because she's currently Gino crazy!
She told me,
"I'm definitely wearing my push-up bra.
I'm done counting on my mother for anything!
I'm going to get some boy love."
"That's so great!" I cluck.

RICHIE O'NEILL

In the morning, the phone rings.
It's not Rachel; it's Richie O'Neill!
He blurts, "If we weren't leaving,
I'd at least take you to the movies."
"What? Leaving? Where're you going?"
"I'm not really sure yet," he says.
"Just packing up.
So if I don't see you in the Bronx,

I'll see you in the next life.
Au revoir."
"Huh?"
"I'll see you sooner or later, *chérie*."
"Richie, you're acting really strange.
Aren't you starting school tomorrow?"
"*Je regret*, Maisie," he says,
pronouncing my name "Maiz-eee."
a) He's never called me before,
and b) he's never spoken in riddles.
I say, "*What* are you talking about?
You can't just quit the Bronx!
You can't leave me here, either!"
"Don't make this hard on me!"
he says,
and before I can get one more word
out of him, he hangs up.
I'm stunned.
The plan was never to survive without Richie.
It's as if one of my organs called
to say goodbye.

YOU'RE SO LUCKY

At our lockers, after orientation,
Rachel, wearing bright-blue eye shadow, says:
"Maisie, it's sad that your dad bolted.
I feel bad for you,
I really do.
Call me whenever you want,
but we're in different
places in our lives now.
I want to spend time with Gino.
Kiki finally joined AA,

so she's either in grad school
or at a Twelve Step meeting.
It's really important that she quits drinking,
so you should probably let her be."
Rachel brushes back her hair
in a flirty, girly way
that I've never seen before.
I start to tell her about Richie,
but she interrupts.
"You do realize that you can be
a little overwhelming, right?
Maybe because you're so brilliant.
You know you're special, right?
And I'm sorry about your nutty family,
but I have my own nutty life.
I have to figure things out."
"Yes, Rachel, I do, but— "
"I envy you, Maisie," she says,
"you're so lucky to love art so much.
I wish I had a passion like that.
I mean, besides John and Jackie.
And Gino, of course."
She smiles and stares at me.
Then she turns and walks away, quickly,
as if I have a highly contagious virus.
I think to myself,
if getting a boyfriend
makes you snooty,
then I don't want one.
But who am I kidding?
I want one.
I want hers.

PHONY PERFUME

Against Rachel's wishes, the next day,
a cloudy, drizzly, futureless afternoon,
I go by Kiki's studio, knock.
Listen to the rain *plink*,
plunk on the garbage cans,
like the distant drumbeat
of a drunken marching band.
Knock again. She lets me in!
"With school and my Twelve Step meetings,
I haven't had a minute to myself lately,"
she explains, drenched in linseed oil.
I inhale it as if it is oxygen.
I like it so much more
than my dad's phony perfume.

HON

I ask her about Nastasia.
Is her gallery for real?
Would she ever want to see my work?
Kiki grabs my hand.
"She's for real.
You're for real.
All of us are for real."
I don't know what to say.

"You're so quiet. What's the matter?"
Kiki says, throwing paint around
like a happy toddler.
I could muster words
if I truly thought she wanted to know.
But I don't.
"Hon?" she asks.
Hon. Like *honey*?
Being called hon is the opposite of
being called dirt.
"Hon?" she says again in her soft,
rumbly cigarette voice, a voice I love.
I hear the gift of that word
as if it were on loudspeakers.
I burst into tears.
Kiki puts her brush down,
touches my arm.
How can I tell her that,
in one syllable,
in one single word,
she's told me who I am.

IT'S EASIER TO CRY IN THE RAIN

Kiki sits me down,
doesn't reach for her cigarettes,
instead takes my hand, says,
"Let's just listen to this downpour together, okay?
It's easier to cry in the rain.
I'm a crier, too," she whispers.
"Frankly, Maisie,
I wish there was more crying.
But folks think once they start,
they'll never be able to stop."
She brings me water.
Then asks about my father.
"You need him," she says,
"even though he's imperfect."
"Imperfect? Seriously?"
"Okay, he's a jerk!
But you love him."
I start to protest, but my chest cramps
as if it might explode.
"You can't stay with your mother, honey.
I'm afraid for you.
She's not in good shape."

FURY

I let those words sink in,
"not in good shape."
"But my dad makes me furious."
"Fury's fine!" says Kiki. "I love fury!"
Somehow this makes me laugh.
"Is there an emotional menu?" I ask.
"Something like that!" says Kiki.
"Promise me you'll think about
talking to your dad."

Rachel clumps in, soaking wet.
When she sees me, her mouth drops.
"Maisie needed to talk," Kiki rushes to say,
and almost sounding guilty.
"Let's all get hot chocolate."
"Not thirsty!" Rachel bellows.
"I'm glad I have a boyfriend.
I don't need either one of you!"
She storms out.
I run after her.
"I didn't get to tell you,
Richie is leaving!"
"Maybe that's why you seem out of it!"
she says.
"I'm not out of it!"
I shout in a way
that makes me sound out of it.
The rain stops exactly at that moment.

SAD NEWS

At school,
Rachel avoids me at our lockers.
In the cafeteria, I say,
"Rache, I miss you.
Why can't we hang out?"
She scrunches up her nose
as if the sentence smells bad.
Then she stops and sends me softer eyes.
"Sorry, I can't. I have a date with Gino.
Don't look so downcast.
Maybe tomorrow?"

Peter Collins sits down next to us,
leans into us and asks if we've heard.
"Heard what?"
"About your pal, Richie," says Peter,
then gulps down his pizza.
"My father's an accountant,
but he's also the super
of Richie's building—
he was there when Richie and his father
had a huge fight," he pauses.
"Deadly," he adds, and reaches for a napkin.

IN THE HEAD

"They were in the hallway.
Richie's dad was demonstrating karate moves.
Mr. O'Neill got really tough on Richie.
The old man began to scream.
It got out of hand.

Then Richie freaked
and kicked his dad in the head!
In the head!
Mr. O'Neill was taken to the hospital.
Concussion. Serious!
The police came, but Richie had vanished.
They're looking for him.
They even questioned *me*!"
He stares at us without blinking.
Now I feel myself turning Richie O'Neill–pale,
ghost white, strangely opalescent,
the walking-confused.

REALLY WANTED

I recall Richie's "sooner or later" phone call.
I wish he would have said more.
Or that I'd made him explain!
I would've told him
we were supposed to be unhappy together!
Until one day, with any luck,
we weren't. Unhappy that is.
But nobody was supposed to
get in trouble with the police!
I guess his dad figured out he was leaving.
What's there to say?
Young Richie, crazy about trains and planes
then poetry, *la langue française,*
is off somewhere.
I won't pass him dreaming on his bench.
He won't punch out any boys for me.
No more inscrutable James Joyce notes.

Is he in trouble?
Where did he disappear to?

BECAUSE OF RICHIE

When school gets out,
I seem to be unable to rise up
off my chair.
Shock?
Rachel saunters by me, then says,
"You look awful!"
"Because I'm guilty! It's *my* fault!
I didn't ask him enough questions.
I thought he and his father were getting along.
My mother's right about me,"
I moan.
Rachel takes my elbow, helps me up.
"Your job wasn't to save him.
You can barely save yourself."
I'm wobbly.
My stomach gurgles loudly.
"Jeez! You should probably come with me
and Gino," she says, so softly and kindly
that the region of my heart comes alive.
"And, anyway, Mr. O'Neill might recover,"
she adds. "He might be fine."
In a daze me and my wretched self
follow Rachel out the door.

AFTERSCHOOL

It's 2 P.M. and Rachel, Gino, and I
head to Fordham Road.

They walk ahead of me
mumbling, sometimes giddily,
sometimes somberly.
I hear her recount the Richie mystery
as we head to the usual spots:
Jay's Coffee Klatch, the corner store.
Finally, we're chewing Chiclets,
sitting across from the subway overpass
watching the commuters.
I take out a pencil and try to sketch Gino's profile.
He has this almost-mustache growing in
and hazel eyes
and really thick, dark lashes
that remind me of a sexy ad for cigarettes.
He could sell anything.
I think to myself, if Gino was the pitchman,
I'd probably start chain-smoking!

ON

I'm thinking about Richie,
worried about his father.
Will he survive, and if not,
does that mean Richie's a murderer?
Somewhere my brain decides
the way to cope is
to become upbeat, entertaining
so I won't explode.
Suddenly I'm talking,
putting on a show,
making my parents' relationship
into a routine.
Telling how,

when my mother got a speeding ticket
my dad said, "When you go in front of the judge
say only two words: *traffic school*!"
She asked, "Shouldn't I explain that I felt sick?"
"'Traffic school!' That is all you say."
"He'll think I'm an idiot, Joe!"
"Doesn't matter, Judith,
say nothing except 'traffic school.'"
My mother almost threw a plate at his head.
Then she went to court.
The judge asked,
"How long have you been driving?"
She said, "Traffic school, traffic school."
The judge looked at her as if she were an idiot.
Then he gave her traffic school!
She was furious that my father was right!
Then, maybe on purpose,
she almost failed traffic school!
Gino starts clapping!

FUN

There's too much energy inside of me!
I need a cosmic benediction.
Someone or something,
to make up for the ditch inside of me.
For my guilt.
Richie was always there for me.
I took him for granted.
Is that the kind of person I am?
So I keep going and going.
Gino tells Rache, "She's funny!"
"Yeah," Rache agrees, "she cracks me up."

She tosses me an unhappy look.
"We should all hang out from now on."
Gino smiles at me.
"Yeah," says Rache, "we really should,"
and looks even more miserable.
I stuff my Gino drawing in my pocket.

MINE

When he leaves, I say,
"Rachel, I don't know what came over me.
I know I was too much. I'm sorry."
She juts out her chin, almost touching mine.
"You infiltrate my life,
but still I invite you along
because I feel sorry for you.
And look what you do:
You try to take everything,
everyone that's mine!
Well, you're not getting Gino!"
She walks away.

SEE YOURSELF

"Hey, Rachel," I call after her,
"I was out of my mind.
I didn't mean to. Honest.
You have to believe me."
Rachel stops in her tracks, then charges me.
"You *did* mean to!
Why don't you even see yourself?
Look in the mirror!

My family is not yours.
You don't even look related!
Your hair is different from ours.
Your skin is different.
Observe!"
She pivots and flounces off, turns the corner.
I'd like to run after her.
But it hits me hard: She's right!
No matter what I want,
I'm not a part of her family.
Only Richie knows how I feel,
needing so much, too much,
wanting people, things
that aren't ours.

GOOD ENOUGH?

Nastasia, Kiki's friend, sends me a brochure
for her gallery
with a note that asks me
if I'm still painting.
I write:
Dear Nastasia, I'm always drawing,
in my house, at school, everywhere.
I'm working mostly with dark colors.
I hope not too depressing.
My friend Richie disappeared,
but he's somehow lurking in my charcoal.
I draw his face from memory.
I try for a brighter palette,
but it turns muddy.
I'm making art to find my friend.
And myself.

FLORIDA VACATION

My grandma is still on her Florida vacation.
I love going to her apartment,
one stop on the Castle Hill line.
I enjoy the subway.
There are all kinds of people,
every color of skin.

I like watching humanity riding the trains.
I draw them, their worried looks,
their worn shopping bags and briefcases,
their jittery kids, unfashionable coats,
looking as if being in New York
was a punishment
they could scarcely manage to bear.

Inside my grandma's apartment,
I feel settled to be with her things,
which to me have an echo
from a long time ago.
My grandmother was young once.
I've seen proof!
Old pictures from the old country.

I feel welcomed here.
This sense of belonging is the opposite
of the flavor in my house.

THE EMPIRE

But today I'm not in the mood
to stick around.
Too guilty to be at peace.
One good friend was probably all Richie needed.
It should have been me!
And it wasn't.
I give the ferns water, spray the succulents,
pick off the dead leaves,
lock the door,
push the elevator button,
ready to cart my burdens home.

IS THAT YOU?

Someone says, "Maisie? Is that you?"
I whip around.
"You don't live here, do you?"
Gino asks, then continues,
"I do! On the top floor!"
He smiles as if I've made his day
by bumping into him in the outdated lobby.
I don't believe in fate.
But this must be fate.
What is wrong with me?
My solar plexus is lighting up
as if there were rocket fuel shooting up my spine,
and all I can think of
is getting closer to him.
Red light! Alarm!
Do not pass go!
He's Rachel's guy!

GREAT POET

"You look upset," he says.

"Richie was my friend," I say.

"I let him down."

"Are you sure? I heard it was really about his father.

Do you want to hear from a great thinker?"

Gino closes his eyes before I can answer.

"And if it is a care you would cast off,

that care has been chosen by you

rather than imposed upon you."

"You think I'm just deciding to worry?" My voice trembles.

"That's what Gibran is saying."

Gino takes a wisp of hair covering my eye

and carefully brushes it aside.

"But it's natural to worry, Gino."

"Maybe natural, but not necessary, Maisie."

But as serious and somber as Gino and I are,

the air is tense, intense, present tense, future tense,

and before I know it, he's asked

to see my grandmother's apartment,

and before I know it, we're there, alone,

and I'm showing him my grandma's needlepoint.

DA VINCI

But Gino's not interested in sewing,
no, he's interested in making out,
which is exactly what I'm interested in.
We're on the couch,
heating up the living room,
tongues everywhere,
hands crawling under clothes,
desperate somehow
to change the laws of physics
and be in the same exact place
at the same exact moment.
There is almost no point in objecting.
It's as if this encounter was already scripted
the first time we laid eyes on each other.
Inevitable. Necessary.
Lacking in free will.
That would explain why
my blouse is half off, right?
Why Gino is bare-chested;
his torso is like a Michelangelo statue,
smooth and perfect.
Rachel's face appears
in my head.
She's screaming. Apoplectic!
I wipe this out of my brain.
Later maybe I'll care but not now,
now I'm just hormones, excitement,
one horny, desperate, despicable girl.
Plus I'm busy thinking,
maybe this is it.
The day someone finally loves me.

THE TRIBE SPEAKS

I'm face up on the couch.
We're both making sounds
I've never heard before;
these deep utterances come from somewhere hidden,
half human, half animal.
The sounds of pure wanting,
if wanting had its own music.
My body has never been so alive.

Beyond Gino's beautiful eyes,
so close to mine,
I spot old black-and-white photos
Grandma has hung on the wall.
My ancestors.
The brown-eyed Hungarians,
in their starched flowered dresses
and stiff wool suits, are frowning.
From inside their antique picture frames,
they're glaring down at me.
Fiercely. Furiously inflamed.
With heartfelt disapproval, horrified!
Their grimaces tell me
that they're completely against this idea
of me practically getting naked
with this boy I hardly know.
Rachel's boyfriend, no less!
What is wrong with you? they shout silently.

I want to ignore them.
Nevertheless, my great-grandmother
is transmitting to me
how she met my great-grandfather escaping the pogroms,

how peasants set the whole town on fire,
trying to kill them as they fled.
Their lives were in danger.
Yet she and my great-grandfather still took it slow!
Had self-respect!
How could I,
the fruit of their nearly impossible escape,
give myself away so easily?
They're screaming, "Stop right now!
Put your clothes on, shana madela!"
And what about Rachel?
Their collective opinion douses me with fear.

I'M RACHEL'S FRIEND

I wriggle away from Gino.
"This is wrong. I can't, I just can't!
And you can't. We can't!"
"Don't do this to me!"
Gino purses his pink puffy lips, says:
"You had to know what I felt about you!"
I point to the wall of Hungarians.
"They're my ancestors!
I'm not playing hard to get.
They won't let me!"

"Just relax." He pulls me to him again.
His fingers entwine with mine.
I peel them off and break away.
"Relax? Nothing about this is relaxing!"
"Not yet . . . ," he says.
"Give me another few minutes."
"It's my grandmother's apartment!"
I argue. "Richie's gone!

Inside, I'm just a big, vacant lot.
You don't want to know me.
Anyway, I'm Rachel's friend!
Her best friend! Except for you!"

He's busy pulling on his shirt.
"Don't be mad at me. Please. *Please*, Gino!"
I grab my blouse, button it up,
try to think of what else I can say,
but he's fast, and the next thing I know,
the door snaps shut
and he's gone, leaving me flat.
I sit down to catch my breath.
I look up again at my ancestors,
decide to hang with them for a while
to see what else they might want to teach me.
I really need to ask Grandma more
about those stern faces
with so many opinions
in the picture frames on her wall.

HIS FAULT

Gino is the one who started it, not me.
He's the one who gave me a copy of *The Prophet*
by Kahlil Gibran the very next day;
he's the one who quoted it:
"Love possesses not nor would it be possessed;
For love is sufficient unto love.
Love has no other desire but to fulfill itself."

He's the one who leaned against my locker
like a *rebel without a cause*,
and asked me to meet him

in front of the cemetery, saying he needed
to talk about something
(which I figured had to be Rachel).
He's the one who
placed his black leather bomber jacket
on my shoulders,
then put his face near mine,
nibbled my cheek,
said he had a thing for girls
with a wicked sense of humor,
long legs, and small ears.

IT WAS ALL HIM

He's the one who tells me stories of woe,
how he was backward in middle school
and still has no idea about dating.
I'm the one who says,
"You're dating Rachel!
So stop acting all lost!"
He's the one who says,
"Don't be fooled,
my cool is all just an act."
I'm the one who wants to comfort him
but know I shouldn't
and then I do, just a little.
I'm the one, when I tell him Rachel
is my absolute best friend
even if currently she is mad at me
and isn't talking to me,
who says he should stop.
He's the one who says Rachel is possessive,
and anyway, she misunderstands;

he likes her a lot, really, she's a great girl,
a lot of fun and smart, but that is all.

Well maybe it isn't all,
but whose fault is it
if he and I are the ones
who are destined to belong together.
He's the one who quotes Gibran again to make his point:
"Love gives naught but itself
and takes naught but from itself."
I'm the one who lets him talk like this,
but he's the one who gives me a kiss
that lasts longer than the dead people
entombed in the cemetery.
It's all him.

STUPID KID

When I get back, it's almost six
and there's no food in the apartment.
There's a note from my mother:
Davy and I are at dinner.
I'm hungry. I make toast.
But I don't want toast.
I find some change
and walk to the pretzel store.
Frank sees my face
and hands me two extra sticks.
He wipes his eyes
to pretend he has a cold.
But I can tell,
it's not a cold at all.
"Sorry, Maisie.

I heard about Mr. O'Neill."
We both gulp down air.
And we chew, absorb the salt,
don't say another word.

When I get home, Davy whispers,
"My room. Now!"
He hands me a soggy half of a corned beef sandwich.
"She's crazy!" he says.
I eat near his messy closet.
His sneakers have a mushroom odor.
But the corned beef is stronger.
The main thing is, for once,
my brother came through!

I COULD SMELL HIM.

"I have a crush on a boy,"
I whisper to Davy.
"So even if Judith starves me,
I'll live on love."
"I hate gym class," he says.
"Everyone's waiting to be chosen
for a baseball team.
Pablo stands so close to me.
He smells nice, like the beach.
I love the beach," he says.
"Then Stu Malcolm,
one of the captains, says,
'Dave, play outfield.'
At bat, Pablo gives me a salute,
then thwacks that ball
out of the schoolyard.

I think he did it for me!"
"I'm not sure what you're saying, Davy."
"Just that I like Pablo," he mumbles.
"Davy," I say,
"everybody has those strange moments,
even me, when you don't know who you like."
"I know who I like," he says.
"I like Pablo. That's the problem."
I'm speechless.
He sighs.
"I had to tell someone."

I look at my brother,
gratified that he trusts me but worried in general.
"You have to be who you are,"
I finally manage.
His face doesn't really change.
"I guess these are your teenage years,"
I add moronically.
Cluelessly. Stupidly.
"I'm only twelve," says Davy.
Then my heart breaks a little.

TOO LATE

I'm the one who tries to stop it.
Gino's the one who says
that I have the softest skin
he's ever touched.
He's the one
whose tongue makes me believe
that maybe life can be sweet.
Still, I'm the one who says

she can't live with herself
if she ever sees him again.
He's the one that says, "Too bad.
Because I'm gone on you,
so it's really way too late."
And he's right; it is too late.

I am Molly Bloom.
"I asked him with my eyes to ask again yes . . .
then he asked me would I yes to say yes . . .
put my arms around him yes and drew him down to me . . .
and his heart was going like mad
and yes I said yes I will Yes."

SHOPPING

There's a note stuck in my locker.
I need to buy dungarees.
Come with me to pick them out. —Gino
I write him: *You're Rachel's boyfriend!*
I'm sorry if I gave you the wrong idea.
I would hate myself
if I did this to her.
Slip it in his locker.
At 3 P.M. he finds me.
"Correction. I am Rachel's friend.
You are Rachel's friend.
Which means we have something in common!"
he says. "And anyway,
what kind of friend avoids you
when you're dealing with a family like yours?
Huh?"

NEVER COMES TO MIND

Rebecca O'Neill,
Richie's sister, bumps into me in the hallway,
freezes me with a stare.
"You're Maisie, right?"
I barely nod. She blurts out:
"Here! I found this in Richie's backpack."
She thrusts an envelope into my hand.
"And no, I didn't read it!"
She turns and runs away.
What is it about this family
and shoving notes at you?
I want to shout,
I don't want this.
I don't want to read about
some puppy-love confession.
But the letter is stiff in my hand.
I'm not sure if I'll ever want to open it.
Never comes to mind.

GIRLFRIEND-BOYFRIEND STYLE

I'm lying to my best friend
when she finally asks me
to hang out with her.
Bald lies, insincere words
tumble out of my mouth
as if I was the poet laureate of deceit.
"I can't.
I want to look over my paintings and drawings
to send to Nastasia.
She's showing the work of young artists in the fall.

It's so important to me."
I half hope to choke on my words.
But Gino and I
are at the store outside of Parkchester,
which we choose—without saying it out loud—
to make sure Rachel won't see us.
My fantasy is that
we're actually a couple,
shopping together, girlfriend-boyfriend style.

Gino's trying on low-rider Levi's.
His hips are slim and sexy.
I want jeans, too.
Gino says, "Try on a pair for girls."
I'm so jazzed:
We're going to have matching Levi's!
Which I can never wear.
If Rachel saw, that'd be the end.
How can you feel awful and wonderful
at the very same time?

HIS HANDS ARE FOOD

We're in my grandmother's empty apartment,
this time not by accident.
Gino's hungry hands are everywhere,
stroking my arms,
touching my face, lifting my sweater.
His palms are warm, but more than that,
they give me an answer to the eternal question:
Will anyone ever love me?
His sweet touch tells me the answer is yes,
definitely yes.
His hands are some kind of food for me.

I take off my sweater,
let him unhook my bra,
feel my breasts, cup them, kiss them.
My breathing, his breathing are synchronic,
our own private percussion.
All I want is to be closer to him.

I WILL LIE

If I ever confide about this to anyone,
I'll say I resisted, said "no"
for hours and hours,
asked all the right questions, like:
Do you really like me? Be honest.
But it's not the truth. I won't ask,
because there is no caution in me.
Caution is for people who can afford it.
In me there's only exhilaration,
craving, the urgency to be filled up.
Gino. Gino. Gino.

GREEN TRAFFIC LIGHT

I'm mumbling, "Yes, yes, yes,"
and the wetness between my legs
is another yes and his hand is there
and I want him.
I thought I'd be frightened,
but I am one big, blazing green traffic light,
telling me to go, go, *go!*
I want this to happen.
I moan, he moans, we moan,
this conjugation of thrill and connectedness

has its own language.
I don't know how long we're like this,
the bed, the walls, the entire place
is moving with us and, I bet,
so is the street.
I hope nobody notices
the earthquake we're creating.
Will there be a tidal wave,
will we all go under the stupendous power
of this heat between us?
Will anyone survive?

THIS IS LOVE

When we're body to body, I think,
he loves me. This is love.
I can live now.
Relief. Tears. Primal belonging.
Will I always need him
to make me feel this?
I hope not.
It's dangerous to rely on Gino,
only a teenager.
And anyway, I don't want to give away
that much of me.
It's too much to give to anyone
and too much for anyone to take.

WAY OFF

That night, Rachel calls me.
She says she misses me!
I'm relieved. But nervous.
Of course I'm nervous.
I deserve to be shot.
"Can you believe, Maise,
I haven't heard from Gino
outside one brief phone call!
He was supposed to model for me again.
He says he loves my drawings of him.
He told me his mother
was taking him away for the weekend.
Something's off, Maisie, *way* off!
Don't you agree?"
"I guess so . . . ," says the breathless hypocrite
on the other end of the phone.

So I drop by her house
and listen to her Gino theories
while I braid her hair.
It's the least I can do.
We slow dance to the radio,
singing the Patsy Cline song.
"Oh crazy
For thinking that my love could hold you . . .
I'm crazy for trying
And crazy for crying
And I'm crazy for loving
you."

★ ★ ★

But really what's crazy
is how I'm letting this boy
become everything to me.
What's crazy is
how I'm lying to my best friend.

LOVING EYES

Gino, Gino, Gino, everything is Gino.
I see his face everywhere,
hear his solemn, low voice,
see his eyes watching me.
My heart finally stops howling
as if the wind could pass right through it.

CRAPPY PERSON

Gino has a whistle that sounds like a bird.
When I hear it,
I sneak out the back door at all hours,
but first I stuff the bed with pillows
so if Judith looks in, she'll think I'm there.
But she never does.
I know this because she'd surely notice
the lumpy bed
was not really in the shape of a person.

I don't feel bad that I meet Gino,
that I get naked
in his father's car,
listening to the Everly Brothers sing
"All I Have to Do Is Dream,"
that we're doing what we're doing.
That I never want to stop.

BONDED PAPER

A letter from Nastasia!
It's embossed in gold and on heavy bonded paper.
It screams important!
It is! It's an invitation to a gallery show!
Wait. It's for last year's show!
But on top of it is a hand-scribbled note:
We'd like to show your work
in this year's Up-and-Comers Exhibition.
Please let me know if you'd like to participate.
Up-and-Comers, not Losers and Louses!
My art, in New York City with real artists
in a gallery on Madison Avenue!
It's the best day of my life!

I run outside to find Richie.
Stupid girl. Richie's gone!
He hasn't come back.
He will never know what this means to me.
I'm not about to call Rachel.
When you can't share joy,
you have to wonder
how long will it continue to *be* joy
before it eventually becomes a fire
you have to smother?

CONSIDERATE

Rachel and I bump into each other
in the girls' bathroom.
She squeals, "I hardly see you anymore!
Did your mother finally have a personality lobotomy?
Did she become . . . nice?"
I lie. "You need Kiki to yourself, that's all."
So I come off as a martyr.
Rachel smiles and says:
"I didn't realize
you could be so considerate!"
Then she whispers,
"Did you hear about Janet?
She missed her period twice!
I would kill myself!"
"At least now Janet doesn't have to worry about
losing her virginity," I say.
"Are you kidding me?"
says Rache. "She's officially a slut!"
I hold on to the sink
to steady my fool self.
This afternoon, I'll go to the pharmacy
and buy condoms.
Or maybe I'll steal them.

PAPER BAGS

I discover notes written on torn brown paper bags
in my sock drawer.
They have words like
haunting, irreverent, loquacious. Yearning.
You can make all kinds of sentences

out of them, put *variable* next to *sad*,
next to *periwinkle, remote* near *spit*.
I ask Davy if they're his.
He yells, "It's none of your business!"
Grabs them out of my hands.
So they are his.
One of them had *Pablo*
written in millions of different letterings.
"I had to hide them, that's all,"
he says.
I want to ask, so you love Pablo?
I understand. I love someone, too.
Isn't love amazing?
But I don't.
One confused, lovesick person
in the family is all I can handle.

WHAT A JERK

Because I don't want Rachel or Kiki
to be suspicious, the day after I run into Rache,
I do sleep over at their house.
But being there isn't like before.
My body aches for Gino all night long.
I wish I could share with Rachel
what this pulsing aliveness I feel
is like, be able to tell her
that Gino is my medicine.

Once in a while, Rachel mentions
how weird it is that he pursued her,
hot and heavy, panting like a thirsty dog,
then dropped her cold.

"What a jerk!" she says.
I tsk-tsk
as if to say, yeah, strange,
but then, you know . . . boys . . .
She pledges that she'll wait
until the summer before college
to have another boyfriend,
that she wants to go away
and leave someone behind
because it's so romantic.
I say, "Yeah, me too.
Exactly how I want to do it."
One day she's bound to find out,
but I have no idea what else to do.
Except break up with this throb of a boy.
But I can't.

PRACTICALLY MARRIED

It's been exactly one month
since the first time with Gino.
I carry around the dog-eared paperback of *The Prophet*.
It's so inspiring. And deep.
How many boys
would even open a book like it?
"When love beckons to you, follow him . . ."
Move over, James Joyce!

It's as if Gino and I are practically married.
It's our anniversary!
We're going to celebrate.
But not at my grandma's
because she's returned from Miami.
I pray she doesn't sniff the lust

we left blanketing her bedroom.
But lucky for us,
Gino's father is out of town tonight.
Gino will pick me up.
We'll have his apartment to ourselves.
I'm dressed, navy sweater, shampooed hair,
cute shoes, a touch of mascara.
I've been ready since five thirty.
But now it's getting late: It's almost nine;
there's no whistle, no phone call.
What if something happened to him?
What if he's in trouble?
My life would be over!
I force myself to recheck my algebra homework
until ten.
At eleven, I change into my old jeans.
I'm jittery, too jittery.
I sneak out down the back stairs
and fast-walk to Gino's
through the mostly empty Bronx streets,
no one in sight,
just litter and bikes
and general lovesickness.

GRANDMA'S BUILDING

Even though it's uphill,
I get there in ten minutes.
Buzz the super's and my grandma's.
They both ask, "Who is this?"
"Oops, I pushed two buttons by mistake."
They both let me in.
I ride up to Gino's on the top floor

and knock. And knock.
"Who is it?" he shouts.
I'm so relieved,
but when the door opens,
I'm the opposite of relieved.
Gino, his shirt unbuttoned,
stares at me as if I'm from another galaxy.
"Shit!" he says. "Shit. *Shit!*"
No poetry tonight.
"Are you drinking?" I ask,
not the real question.
A girl's voice.
"Who's knocking at this hour?"
Gino steps outside into the hallway,
purple-faced, trying to find speech.
Then, he splutters:
"For it is your friend to fill your need,
but not your emptiness."
I yell: "Talk like a normal person, Gino!"
I've seen lots of movies.
I know there's going to be a lame speech,
and whatever words he's concocting
are ones I don't want to hear.

MAMALEH

I run downstairs to the second floor
and pound on my grandma's brass knocker.
I can hear the TV on in her bedroom;
at least I didn't wake her up.
Her slippers shuffle to unlock the door.
I push past her.
"So that vas you on the buzzer?

Dank God! I thought I vas going to be robbed."
She closes her faded lavender robe,
sits on the couch, pats it.
"Mamaleh," she says, sits.
"You look terrible!"
I whisper,
"Don't ask me any questions, please."
"Okay," she says. "Maybe later we'll talk."
Probably not, I think to myself.
My heart is locked up,
like there's a death in the family.
Somehow, a tear falls on me.
It can't be mine,
because I swear my eyes are dry.
"I am truly an idiot, a fool!" I mumble.
"And one thing I know, Grandma:
Life is harder for idiots and fools."
"We're all idiots and fools," she says,
puts her arm around my shoulders.
After a while my late-bloomer grandma
manages to soothe me and I fall asleep.

BEGGAR

When I awaken, I face the truth:
I deserved what happened.
I stole my best friend's boyfriend.
I was arrogant,
thinking Gino would treat me
differently than he treated Rachel.
I'm so ashamed.
Meanwhile, my mute, urgent,
riled-up body, wild with longing,

thinks that any minute he'll come back
and be with me, touch me,
feed me with words and tenderness.
My stupid body is truly a bigger beggar
than my heart.
I tell Grandma a little, then make her promise
not to say anything to my mother.
I wish I could have a conversation
with Rachel,
one where we shake our heads
and say "boys . . ." and roll our eyes
with fake disgust,
then listen to the Everly Brothers sing
"All I Have to Do Is Dream . . ." and promise to always be best
friends,
promise to never let any dumb boy crush
get between us,
because aren't we practically sisters?

LIKE DIRT

Gino doesn't even bother to call me!
Now I realize I can't trust myself to tell
if a human being is decent or not.
He's treating me like dirt.
And I am.

NOT THAT KIND OF GUY

Three days later, I find a scribbled letter
in my locker.
I was getting too close to you.
I don't want a real girlfriend.
I love you, Maisie, so much,
but I don't want to love you.
Funny.
There aren't any Kahlil Gibran poems
for those sentiments.
Gino has written: *I have this bad habit*
of falling for someone
then leaving them;
I'm just like my no-good father,
who's had three wives.
Don't worry,
I won't tell anyone how far we went,
I'm not that kind of a guy.
He adds, *Please forgive me,*
I'm never going to amount to anything . . .
and a lot of other pitiful-sounding sentences.
I have to stop reading,
because after all of that, it seems
the real reason he wrote the letter
was to make *me* feel sorry for *him*.
What a jerk: him.
What a bigger jerk: me.

ROSES

Rachel calls to invite me over
for Kiki's birthday.

I have to say yes
or Rachel will be suspicious.
I'm too depressed to go out,
let alone to a party, even for Kiki.
I have to rally.
I cut a rose
from my mother's fire escape rosebush.
She says I have no business stealing her prettiest buds,
harangues me with the history of her cherry-red Starfires,
the water they need,
the tender-loving care
and special food,
until I want to take one
and scratch her face with the thorns.
She loves roses more than humans.
"It's a present," I keep muttering,
"for someone who's been very nice to me."
I say the word *nice* as if has thirteen syllables.
"I'll tell her the rose is from you,"
I offer. "Okay?"
"Okay," she says, softens, and even adds
"just don't stay out all night,"
then offers to drop me off at their house.
Did that just happen?
Is my mother changing?

FEEL PROUD

We pull up to Rachel's building.
I hesitate, thinking Judith
probably wants to be included.
I force myself to ask:
"Want to come in and say hi to Kiki?"

She's flustered, then says,
"Not the way I look, no."
How I wish, with all my heart,
that I wanted her to come in;
that I could feel proud;
that I could stand next to my mother
with gratitude or affection
or a sense of connection,
hold her hand; that we'd be a team
and I could bring her into my world.
But instead, I'm relieved.
"Well, maybe another time,"
I say vaguely, then run inside
and hand Kiki the rose.
A thorn scratches her arm.
"I can't believe I just hurt you,"
I gasp.
"Beauty always seems to involve pain,"
she says philosophically.
How can you not love someone who's so gracious?

KIKI'S BIRTHDAY

There is the delicious smell of beef stew.
Ken calls out hi from the kitchen.
Jake and Jonathan gleefully chase each other
around the table,
shouting out threats of zombie attacks.
Rachel rolls her eyes, older-sister style.
All I can think about is when Rachel's eyes
will land on my face.
She'll pause, then say, "You look different!"
She's going to probe, too.

"You're not a virgin anymore, is that it?"
She's going to ask, "When? Who?"
and "Did you like it?"
Luckily I'm no longer glowing.
Or if not Rachel, then Kiki.
I can just see her tilt her head,
touch her bracelets, say, "Hmm.
You look different, Maisie.
Wait, I bet I know!
You've been having sex, you little minx!"
Kiki has insight.
Too much insight.

UNEVENTFUL NIGHT

"Happy birthday, Kiki," I mumble.
She smiles. Her lipstick has made
a small stain on her lips.
Her lace blouse is a little crooked,
so I wonder if maybe she's already begun
to celebrate with unknown bottles of wine.
But I relax.
I'm being paranoid.
They may be intuitive,
but they're not psychic!
I help Ken get the food onto the table,
hoping it will be an uneventful night.
Kiki only drinks water.
I wish I could drink some wine.
Getting a little buzz
would help quell the anguish.
But for once, nobody is drinking!

ACTING NUTS

Kiki tells us about some of the mistakes
she's made with her studies.
She has clients and a supervisor,
but yesterday she told her patient
"Nancy, you're acting nuts,"
which her supervisor informed her
is not how you speak to someone
who needs help.
Still, she says, they have confidence
she'll make a good therapist one day
because she truly cares about other people
and is a recovering alcoholic,
which they are very impressed with.
The recovering part, that is.

WHAT MUD?

She says her professors get that
she isn't afraid to step in the mud.
"What mud?" I ask.
"The mud of deep emotional stuff.
Kiki loves the mud," Rachel adds.
"She holds it against me
that I don't, right, Mom?
You think I'm not that interesting
because I'm not tormented."
Kiki takes a drag on her cigarette.
"I made it my life's purpose to raise kids
who were not tormented," she says,
a little annoyed.
"So sue me."

RAISED EYEBROWS

Kiki stabs her cigarette butt out.
"Maisie, it's been so long since we've seen you!
Why don't you catch us up with your life?"
Everyone is staring at me now.
"Not much to say.
You know, school. Homework . . ."
These people who've been nothing
but kind and helpful to me
all have raised eyebrows;
they all know I'm a big talker.
I'm sweating and clammy.
"You're looking all shiny," says Rachel.
I hear gurgling. It's my stomach.
The beef stew is making it noisy, unhappy.
I push my chair away from the table,
get up just in time to make it into the bathroom,
where I throw up.

Kiki knocks. "You okay?"
"I have to go home," I whimper,
then clean up and open the door.
"I'm sorry," I say to Rachel, Kiki,
the brothers, and Ken.
"It was really good;
I guess I'm just not feeling well.
Don't hate me for messing up your evening."
As if that's what I'm guilty of messing up.

FREAKIER THAN USUAL

I bolt out of there.
Rachel's on my tail,
rides down in the elevator with me.
"You're acting all freaky," she says,
"even more than usual.
What's up with you?"
Her eyelids half close, sniff me out,
sensing something.
"Why don't you want to talk?"
"Can't, Rache, can't!
Don't feel well!"
I run, dash from streetlight to streetlight,
half wishing Gino would drive by,
beg my forgiveness,
say we have to be together,
and half wishing I could run ahead ten years,
skip everything that's facing me right now.
Mostly myself.

RUNNING

Rachel follows me.
Then I hear something fall
out of my pocket;
Gino's copy of *The Prophet*
tumbles down onto the pavement.
Rachel scoops down and picks it up.
"Gino adores this book," she says.
Then she stares at it for a long moment.
"You're hiding something from me, Maisie!
If this was about your mother,
you'd have already told me."
Then she holds the book up
to her nose and sniffs.
"It smells like Gino!" she whispers,
riffles through the pages.
I try to grab it out of her hands.
Her eyes bulge.
"Why do you have his book?"
she screams.
I'm running.
I've never run faster in my life.
"If you went after him— Gino is *my* boyfriend!"
Rachel screams into the night.

THE TRUTH

I make it home, jump into bed,
promise myself never to leave it again.
Rachel saw right through me
like I knew she would.
Footsteps down the hallway.
My door swings open.
Rachel stands there panting, fuming.
"Time to be honest.
Tell me what happened! I have to know!"
"How'd you get here so fast?"
I squeak.
"Kiki drove me.
She wants to know, too."
This is the second-worst moment in my life.
"You're going to hate me,"
I moan miserably.
"It *is* about Gino!" She kicks the bedroom door hard.
It bangs against the wall.
She storms out yelling,
"Stay away from me
and my mother, you creep. Forever!"
I want to tell her something that will make her
my best friend again,
but I don't deserve a best friend.
And there's nothing I can say.

Judith blocks the doorway.
"What's going on, Rachel?"
"What's going *on*?
Ask your daughter.
She stole my boyfriend!

But come to think of it"—Rachel pauses—
"maybe that's because you're such a bitch to her!"

THERAPY

Rachel clamors down the hallway,
slams the front door.
My mother settles into my desk chair,
a boulder of disapproval, says:
"We need to do something about you."
I'd like to say:
We need to do something
about *you*, Mother.
Instead I ask, "Like what?
Cut off my hair? Auction me off?
Send me to the leper colony?"
"What's your fascination with leper colonies?
There are none in the USA.
Therapy. You need therapy, Maisie."
Her voice is as hard as the cement sidewalk outside.
I have so many responses to this.
None of them goes
"Sounds like a good idea!"
I stand up, holler:
"I know! I could run away, like Richie."
She rises off the chair, typhoon-like.
We're facing off in my small bedroom.
"Don't you try to manipulate me, girl.
I'll have you *sent* away. Or put away.
They have places for problem kids like you."
"You just try!" I scream, grab my purse,
bolt out, bang the bedroom door
until it vibrates like an oncoming storm.

Let her stay in my room,
thinking up plans to hurt me.

I HAVE TO

I take refuge in the bathroom.
I remember that in my bag is that note
Rebecca O'Neill gave me weeks ago.
I open the folded-up paper.
Richie wrote *Maiz-eee*
as if he was holding on to my name
and couldn't let it go.
It's been a month since he left.

DAISY GIRL

Maiz-eee!
Maisie, daisy,
you and me, we're not too different,
only you're pretty, ha ha.
I've wanted to tell you that you're pretty.
But I didn't want you to laugh at me.
One day I was going to walk
up to you and say it, "You're pretty."
I'm not a poet. I'm just full of feelings
that I try to keep from pouring
out the front of my freckled Irish face.
I loved it when we went to Safeway
or met and talked in the street.
You smell of daisies.
I can never figure it out
because I never see daisies in the Bronx.

RUN-DOWN HOTEL

Judith screams.
I can't understand what she's saying.
But when I fold up the letter, something has shifted.
That paper had love on it.
Cherishing.
To Richie, I matter.
I feel that in my body,
a certain fullness. And warmth,
but also a sadness
of how much I need those things
and a knowing that
I can't keep letting her tear me up
the way she shredded my homework.
I realize I have to rescue myself.
I return to my bedroom,
pack a blouse, panties, a jacket,
my blue flannel pajamas,
and tiptoe down the back stairs,
out the building.
And walk. And walk.
I leave Parkchester.
Across from the bus stop
there's a run-down hotel
that's been there ever since I can remember.
It's the only one around here,
and because it has a beamed ceiling in the lobby
and a large stone fireplace,
it's considered a historical landmark.
My dad has always kept an open account
for when our cousins come to town.
I pull my hair into a neat rubber band
and march in,

declare that I'm waiting for everyone to arrive,
I'm just a little early for a family reunion.
The woman is suspicious,
but I keep yammering
about how my dad loves this place
how he puts everyone up here at least once a year,
and I flood her with the facts of when it was built
as the Bronx's most-respected lodging,
where Roosevelt once dined.
She gives me the once-over.
Sighs. Shakes her head,
opens her files, finds my dad's name,
and maybe just to shut me up,
gives me a key and shows me to a room
that smells like window cleaner
and looks out at an alley.
I lock the door, splay out on the bed.

FLANNEL PAJAMAS

I feel as if I'm on an ice floe
somewhere in the North Pole,
drifting away from all civilization,
from all connection, all hope.
Then I think, well,
I've always felt this way.
I can remember exactly seven times
when I didn't feel completely isolated
and on my own,
a soldier on an endless battlefield.
So why should I feel sorry for myself *now*?
I jump off the bed, unpack, find my blue flannel pajamas,
lay them out, then run a hot bath

and submerge myself,
scrub leisurely, sing softly, then belt out the lyrics
to "Somewhere" from *West Side Story*:
There's a place for us . . . Because I have to believe
there's a place for me
like the song says.
Finally my fingertips are puckered,
so I take a shower, wash my hair,
dry off with the extra-plush towels,
then climb into my pj's
and think about how
somehow, someday . . . somewhere . . .
my life will be off-limits to my mother.

ANGRY AT LIFE

She will get old and wither, but I will flourish.
My life force is strong!
I remember a dream I keep having:
I'm in an airplane.
Judith is the pilot,
flying under bridges,
between high-rises, out of control, dangerous.
I shoot up out of the nightmare.
I'm a wreck.
I realize I'm angry, angry at life,
life itself for giving me too much to handle.
Couldn't life wait a few years?
No. It had to get me now.

I AM HERE NOW

Kiki says that when she has anxiety attacks,
what works for her is to get air.
So now I open the window,
make sure to look up at the trees
because trees are on my side,
except for the sad, scrawny ones
that need hugs more than I do.
Clouds are on my side, too,
but howling dogs are not,
loud screaming TVs are not,
but I look in another direction
and see a sliver of moon.
Kiki says, "Remember to breathe
and your normal consciousness will return."
Kiki talks about consciousness
deliberately, as if it has more
than three syllables, like it's a destination,
as if everyone's on a train,
a train to consciousness.
I bet Kiki's friends sit around
and talk about consciousness.
Maybe for them it's like a resort,
a place to visit on a long weekend,
pack up, take the dog.
That's where the weather is perfect
and also very calm.
Not like my consciousness.
I try to remember that the main me
is still in here somewhere.
Sometimes, like now, it helps
if I chant under my breath:
"I am here now, I am here now,
I am here now, I am here now."

SLEEP WOULD BE GOOD

Calm down. Think. Just think of a plan!
Where do I go?
Who, besides Richie, likes me, loves me?
Great-Aunt Dalvinka lives alone,
but would she want me there?
Does she love me enough?
Could she understand?
In the morning I might have to beg.
I would have to beg.
A fly buzzes around,
makes a lot of noise,
makes me feel as if there is an unholy presence around,
especially as I hear the electricity buzzing, too.
Sleep would be good,
sleep is my friend, yes,
let me just rest,
so I can forget about the endless archives
of unlucky incidents.

LIAR

Once when my mother was out shopping,
I opened her desk drawer, rifled through receipts,
check registers, old lipsticks,
and discovered a paper with my father's new address.
His phone number, too.
I thought about calling him,
I admit it, I actually dialed his number.
Then I slammed the phone down.
He really had me believing he loved me.
But I'm not stupid.
He lives on East Eighty-Eighth Street.
I wonder if he has a fancy apartment.
With a doorman.
Or a balcony, thick carpets?
How many bedrooms?
Is this only a hideaway for him
and his witless girlfriend?
Does she have kids?
Did he take anything of mine,
any of my drawings? A photo?
How could he have run off like a bandit?!
Why couldn't the coward sit down
and level with me and Davy?

Does he spend his days
worrying about perfume
and the fourth-quarter earnings?
And his nights loving this new person?
Does he ever glance out the window
and look toward the Bronx?

For some crazy reason,
I memorized his number.
But liars, betrayers, and heartbreakers
do not deserve calls
from the people they duped.

OPEN UP

I drift off on the wet pillow.
Then, pounding: loud, insistent, end-of-the-world
pounding on the door.
My heart starts pounding, too,
thumping like a paddleball set.

"Maisie Meyers, are you in there?
Is that you, Maisie? Open up!"
say confident, loud male voices.
"Who is it?" I whimper.
"The police."
How did they find me?
Who told them I was here?
The lady at the front desk?

DISAPPROVING LOOKS

I jump out of my pajamas,
pull on my pants, unlock the door.
Two huge guys with badges, heavy leather holsters
give me disapproving looks.
"Don't arrest me!" I plead.
"You're a minor! You're coming with us!"
"I was just trying to think things through,"
I lamely explain
as they wait for me to finish changing clothes
and grab my bag.
Then they usher me
through a back door and into a police car.
At least they don't put the siren on.
I shiver in the back seat
while they call in.
"She ain't kidnapped or dead,"
says the guy on the walkie-talkie,
all pleased and triumphant.
As if not being kidnapped, not being dead
is all I can hope for.

FILE A REPORT

At the station, my mother, arms crossed,
glares at me.
"*What* is the matter with you?
Don't I have enough to handle without this?"
She turns to the officer.
"My husband abandoned us,"
she says pitifully,
and folds herself onto a wooden chair.
They turn to me,
"Is there a problem at home?"
But I don't want to talk to them.
How can I tell my story
while she's sitting right there?
You can't file a report that you are unwanted.
You can't say,
"I think if my mother saw me
lying in a coffin she'd smile wide,
as if she were on *Candid Camera*."
"I guess I'm just confused," I say.
Judith rolls her eyes,
then, realizing that isn't going to help her case,
she adds "Poor kid," sounding almost kind.
"You know"—she puts a pleasant look on her face—
"teens act out."
She and the officer nod the way adults do
when they bond
over being *so* preternaturally wise about life.

Naturally, they release me to her.
We don't talk in the car.
Now I'm a deader duck than ever before.
Neither Rachel nor Kiki

will talk to me ever again,
which makes me as dead as you can be
and still have blood
running through your veins.

RED EYES

My father has been informed
that I tried to run away.
Legally, he had to be.
He calls the next day and the next,
morning, evening, sends flowers,
which I actually get for once.
I refuse to speak to him.
Two reasons.
I'm too mad for sure.
I also figure if I don't talk to him,
she'll believe that I'm on her side,
and I need her to think that—
to survive.
So I shake my head no
when she thrusts the phone at me.
My father even gets his secretary
to call in her sugary, creepy
"I understand your pain" voice.
No, she doesn't.

THUG

Now Grandma starts coming to dinner
frequently, but she doesn't seem like Grandma.
She talks like a thug
and makes faces like the gargoyles
you see on churches.
Every other sentence is "that cheat,"
or "that louse," or
"that no good son of a . . ."
I've lost five pounds because I can't eat
and listen to her,
and anyway,
I'm the one who is mad at him,
so what is she complaining about?
But I look out my window
when they think I'm in bed.
I'm waiting to see if Richie will return.
Because, I mean, he's only eighteen.
Where did he go?

One night Mr. O'Neill returns.
He walks into his building.
Walks by himself, no cane, no wheelchair.
Doesn't even limp.
So Richie didn't kill him!
Where are you anyway, Richie?

I KNOW YOU'RE AWAKE

There's nobody to speak to
in this dreaded place.
It's like being on death row:
Something awful is hanging over my head.
One day I'll walk straight into Davy's room,
say, "I know you're awake,"
sit on his bed, and apologize
for having resented him
since the exact minute he was born.
We have the same genes.
I wonder how much of him is lost
in all the hiding.

TAKE ME WITH YOU

The day comes when I do knock.
He's the one banging his head
in his room,
ruining his brain.
I say: "Hey, watch TV with me.
I'll watch anything you want."
I have to help him.
I stand there, hold my breath.
Finally he says, "Come in."
We don't go to the TV.
We sit and breathe.
"She doesn't like you," he says.
"But I'd rather she hated me
than be on my case.
Next time you run away,
take me with you. Promise, Maisie?"
"Okay, Davy. Promise."

DAVY'S ROOM

New, awful development:
My mother is after Davy now.
"Where've you been?"
she hollers whenever
he comes home late.
"Out," he says vaguely.
"Why is a twelve-year-old boy
so secretive?" she hollers.
"Leave me alone. I'm studying!"
He shuts his door.
"I will not accept this behavior," she huffs.
"Go away!"
Davy growls.
"I'm not a stand-in for your husband."
Wow!!! That was brave!
But she doesn't leave him alone.
Instead,
she looks through his underwear drawer,
finds some papers
like the ones he hid in my sock drawer.
"Pablo? Who the hell is Pablo, Davy?"
Davy's mute.
"Maisie, get in here!" she screams.
"Have you ever heard about any of Davy's friends
with that name?"
"There's a Michael,
who he walks to school with,
and Darren, who he calls
to check his homework.
But *Pablo*?"
I think, miracle!

For once it's not me.
Then I think,
why does it have to be either one of us?

MAMA'S BOY

I try to intervene before it gets worse.
I say, "Listen, he's growing up.
You don't want him to turn into a mama's boy."
"I'm the mother!" she screams.
"He's my responsibility!"
"Can you please calm down?
You're out of control," I say.
This is new for me,
sticking my neck out for Davy.
Davy, of course, says nothing.

PRIVACY

"Why're you so upset?" I ask.
She bleats, "*Why?* Why. Are. These. Notes.
Hidden. In. His. Drawer?
Since when does he keep secrets?
Is he writing love notes to a Pablo?"
Davy finally speaks,
his face grim and frozen:
"It's none of your business, Mother!"
"Everything in this house is my business, David!"
"You'd be surprised!" he shouts
uncharacteristically loudly.
"What's that supposed to mean?"
she screams.

"It means you don't know everything
about me and never will.
You should leave, Mother!"

GET OUT OF HERE

"You don't tell me to leave!"
His face is turning barn-fire red.
"Why are you blushing, David?"
Her hands rest on her hips,
always a bad sign.
"I want you to respect me!"
he demands, disturbingly, utterly calm.
"You don't tell me what to do, boy!"
"I hate you!" he hollers, cheeks crimson.
Her hand swings back. *Slap.*
He recoils, covers his face.
"You're getting to be like your sister,"
she says. "Big mistake, buster!"
Slap on his other cheek.
He swings at her.
She tries to grab his hand in hers.
"You're going to be sorry!" she screams,
and lets loose, pounding him
like homemade bread.

ARE YOU CRAZY?

At first I'm immobilized.
These two have never fought. Never *ever*.
Then I plant myself between them.
Next thing I know, I'm down.
My right shoulder hits the nightstand.
I glare at Judith, and out of me comes this:
"Are you crazy? What are you thinking?
We're your *children*!
You're supposed to take care of us,
not torment us!"
Davy helps me back up on my unsteady feet,
then I see he wants to hit her again.
"No, Davy!"
I hold his arm steady.
"You're not angry at us, Mom," I yell.
"You're angry at yourself. Your *life*!"
I throw myself against the door.
Instead of hitting her,
I slam it hard a few times
until the frame makes a cracking sound.
"I'll never be like you!" I sob.

WHAT I GAVE UP FOR YOU

"Be like me?!" she yells.
"You don't even know me.
You've no idea what I gave up for you."
"That's what mothers do!" I say.
"But you couldn't!"
"Here's why." She glowers.
"I never wanted children!
How's that for the truth?
You were both mistakes!"
She turns on Davy.
"What are you looking at?"
"You don't know me, either, Mother,"
he mewls.
"What I know is that no woman
will marry you if you don't change."
"Don't worry. I'm never getting married,"
says Davy. "No thanks!"
"What the hell does *that* mean?"
she screams.
She removes her high-heeled pump
and starts to slam it on my cheek.
"It's all your fault."
Sweat beads are forming
under her makeup.
Davy tries to grab the shoe from her.
So she starts clobbering him
on the head, that same head
that he flings against the wall every night.

HE'S YOUR BABY

"Stop! He's your baby!"
I scream. "You're hurting him!"
I feel the desire to obliterate this woman
who gave me life
and then did all she could
to make sure I had no shot at it.

ON THE FLOOR

Davy and I grab Judith's hands
and hold them behind her back.
I say slowly,
"Control yourself. *Stop!*
You have to stop."
Her eyes flip open as if hit by lightning.
Then she wrangles free and storms out
of Davy's room and into her bedroom.
I hear her muttering,
"Oh God. Oh God!"

CALLING DAD

"I'm calling Dad" are the words I hear
escape from my own mouth
while standing outside her door.
I sound like a prison guard,
measured, sane, defiant.
"Mother, you have to tell him
that we can't stay with you anymore.
We're not safe here.
You know it's true.
I have his number.
Shall I call him, or will you?"

OVER

She emerges, walks to the living room.
Her face is no longer raging.
Distorted, yes, but eerily calm.
Like an automaton,
she picks up the phone,
dials, trembles,
but manages to say:
"Joe, I'm done. It's over.
It has to be over."
She instructs him to get in the car
and drive up here to the Bronx.
I am standing close enough
to hear my father mumble,
"It's late, Jude."
She says, "I know it's late, moron!
That should make you realize this has to happen."
"You're sure?"

His half-asleep voice is so much creamier
than his dad-the-boss voice.
The words fall out of her,
tensely, quietly, deliberately.
"Yes, Joe. I am. I am sure.
You need to take them."
"Okay." He coughs a smoker's cough.
"I'm on my way."

Davy and I pack some stuff.
We're frantic.
Like refugees who will never set eyes
on their homeland again,
we ride the elevator down to the lobby
to wait for the ship that is my father's car
to ferry us across the Harlem River
to a different life.

I STOLE FROM YOU

Dear Rachel,
I know. I know.
You're not speaking to me.
I don't blame you.
But please know
you're the best thing
that happened to me in all my years
in the Bronx.
You lent me your home and your heart
when I needed both so badly.
And what did I do?
I stole from you!
The worst kind of thief.

I don't blame you for hating me.
I realize I have to let you go,
but I can't. Not yet.
So I'm writing to you.
And even though
you won't read my letters . . .
I have to send them anyway.
Did you at least notice the postmark?
It's New York City.
Manhattan!
I had to tell you. We're safe now.

BLAME ME IF YOU WANT

Dear Rachel,
I'm realizing there's no reason
for Davy and me
to go back to the Bronx again.
The Bronx is history.
The Bronx was never good to me.
Or to him.
I'm trying to lose my accent
and my memories, too.
Except for you.

I'm not making excuses,
but after my father left
and Richie disappeared,
I felt I was going under.
It seemed to be life or death.
I thought Gino was somehow necessary
for me to survive.
Stupid! Ridiculous! Despicable!

Selfish, out of control, a jerk of a friend.
A horror show.
I get it would be difficult,
no, impossible to trust me again.
You could call me every name in the book
and it wouldn't begin to describe
how underhanded I was.

DESTINY

Dear Rachel,
It's been three days
since Davy and I became brand-new downtowners.
That first morning,
we woke up on the fourteenth floor
of his building on East End Avenue.
We look down on Gracie Mansion.
That's where the mayor lives!
Light bulb moment.
There might be one potential great thing
about living in Manhattan
if, only if, I could get in
to the High School of Art and Design.
Once your mother told me about it,
I decided that has to be my destiny!
I'm writing in case
you have the tiniest shred of interest.
But why would you?
I know this is a one-way street.

SWANK

You wouldn't believe this, Rachel.
My dad's apartment walls
have fabric on them!
Silk! It's sumptuous, swank.
Mirrors everywhere, a Jewish Taj Mahal.
Dad said, "Kids, Brandy did the decorating.
She has a great eye."
Naturally, Brandy—Dad's girlfriend,
or whatever she is—brightened.
I thought, Dad, of course you'd say that:
Those eyes looked around and found you!
The two of them were standing by the doorway.
He draped his arm around her,
and she sank into him.
I admit it:
I've never seen my mother happy
when my dad touched her.

"We're going to have a nice time together,"
my dad said.
"You bet," Brandy agreed.
"I love you, kids," he added.
I wish I could hear what you'd say about that.
I always cherished what you thought.
But I'm not holding my breath.

I HOPE

So, Rachel,
I told Brandy about
the High School of Art and Design.
The next thing I knew we were in a taxicab
driving down Lexington,
going for a preliminary interview!
Mrs. De Floria, the assistant principal, said
I'll have to show them a portfolio as a kind of audition
to get in next year.
She gave me a list of pieces
to include,
plus essays to write, grades to transfer.
Brandy made sure to tell the vice principal
I'm included in a gallery show
on Madison Avenue.
That's because of Nastasia,
your mom's friend.
Mrs. De Floria's eyebrows rose up.
Smile.

THE LIST

For the portfolio, I'll need
an exterior landscape,
an original graphic design,
a three-dimensional sculpture,
an idea for a toy,
the map of an imagined country,
three figure drawings,
two portraits.
You know I love to draw faces;

they're landscapes to me,
foreign countries of forms,
shapes, and volume.
I lose myself in them.
I love the way a nostril can tell you
someone's haughty or a chin suggests
a certain kind of laziness
or defiance, as if personalities
are inscribed in flesh and bone
for all the world to see.
Nothing on them is random;
all our features are a code!
Who is the artist who figured that out?
Daumier, maybe?
Did you ever think about these things, Rachel?
I miss you so much.
I love your face, your perfect face.

I AM THE MASTER

Rachel, you'd understand better than anyone
how my mother's visage haunts me.
Those cold eyes,
the lips gripping each other,
the severity of her spirit.
I'm drawing to understand her,
I guess, or to stop being afraid.
A pencil in my hand
helps me feel some control.

SLOPPY LINES

My first attempts are totally abstract;
an unknown energy moves my hands.
There's an astonishing motor inside me,
turned on like never before.
Big inhales, exhales,
and I want to sing and I can't sing!
I get so involved, so captured, and honestly,
if Naples Yellow right next to Cerulean
doesn't completely carry you away,
nothing ever will!
I feel what the masters must have felt:
benign delirium!
Giotto, Rembrandt, Matisse, Tchelitchew.
When I meet them in art heaven,
will they talk to me
about light sources
or the meaning of turquoise, please?
Well, I don't really think
I'll land in heaven . . .
Anyway, I don't know how long I've been at it,
but finally I step back.
What I've made is ugly.
But somehow it is also beautiful.

HARD TO EXPLAIN

I picture you at the mailbox,
seeing my letters,
getting annoyed and tossing them out
before you even open them.
Telling your mom
what a complete disaster it was
that you bothered to know me.
Still, I keep writing to you.
The poetry of apology.

COURAGE

Dear Rachel,
Brandy isn't bitchy
if I treat her a certain way
(which means saying a million times a day
how beautiful she is and that
she has a great rack,
which is humongous,
then, ugh, she has to tell me
that my dad loves them, too).
Brandy cooks a great roast duck.
And sometimes comes into my room
and actually talks to me.
I guess I'll put her on probation.

MISS YOU MISS YOU MISS YOU

Dear Rachel,
One last attempt to get through to you:
Enclosed is the invite to the opening
of the gallery show.
If you don't come,
I promise I'll never bother you again.
One more thing:
I got an encouraging letter from Art and Design!

Alone, at night,
I pretend you and I have conversations
and that you're happy for me.
You would be,
if only I hadn't been a total scoundrel.

WHO YOU CAN AND WHO YOU CAN'T HAVE

Dear Maisie,
Can you believe, Gino lives with his mother!
Nobody knows where the dad went!
His perfect family was perfect fiction!
Last week he left a rose at my front door.
Romantic, right?
Then I found out he left roses
for four other girls
at their front doors!
I personally know three of them!
I get it now:
I'm the dense one.
I'm the blind one.
I should've known about him.

But how could I've known about you?
It's tough to be you. I get it.
But it's tough to be anyone.
P.S.
Do not bother looking for me at Nastasia's show.
I won't be there.
Read my lips.
That's a firm promise.

ZIP-A-DEE-DOO-DAH

Dear Rachel,
Look—I guess neither one of us
knows much about boys.
I hope there aren't too many more
Ginos out there.
Brandy says, "Beware."
She's kind of superficial
but maybe also
a little wise about certain things.

Today, my grandma and I
were walking downtown.
The sky was a cheerful, zip-a-dee-doo-dah blue.
She gave me a handmade silk scarf
with the most elaborate,
exquisite embroidery,
which was stitched by her mother,
my great-grandmother Estelle.
When I looked at it, I thought of you.
Which is why I'm sending it.
It's a please-forgive-me-or-at-least-
don't-despise-me-forever gift.

Dear Maisie,
Your mother gave me this letter to give to you.
Doesn't she have your address?
I think it's from France!
Who do you know in France?
Richie? Could it be from Richie?
If it is, I'd like to know if he's okay.
Rachel

I open the letter.
Cher Maisie (pronounced "May-zee"),
Ça va bien. Really. I'm good!
Tres bien, actually.
I'm in Paris!
I walked on the rue where James Joyce lived!
I had to wait to write you
until I knew my father pulled through.
When I first ran off,
I lived with my second cousin, Colin,
until I was able to get a passport.
Then I went to the docks
and hid in the hull of a ship.
I know. I never thought of myself
as adventurous, either.
Yes, they discovered me.
I begged the captain to give me passage.
I said I could teach everyone karate.
I had the best time, Maisie.
My French is improving, vraiment.
I called my mom long distance.
She moved back in.
My dad is going to therapy now.

A miracle.
Write me. Tell me everything.
Je t'adore,
The boy across the way.
R

Dear Rachel,
Yes! The letter is from Richie!
I'll tell you more when I see you.
If I see you. No. When I see you.
Okay, that's asking too much.
Forget I mentioned it.
You can't get arrested for wishing, though, right?
Every day that passes,
there's remorse in every cell of my body.
If I put it on a scale
it would weigh tons and tons.
Maisie

MANHATTAN OPENING

Wearing all black,
well, charcoal black technically—
I look like a New Yorker tonight!
I teased my hair,
then I combed it out.
It was too much!
Then I teased it again.
This went on for some time.
Who, me, nervous?
My father has brought his Polaroid camera.
He posed me standing next to my canvas,
shaking hands with Nastasia,
signing a few brochures,
answering questions for an interview
for *The Gallerist*'s next issue.
Proof that in the middle of a swamp
a lotus will bloom.
A takeaway from Kahlil Gibran.
Well, it's proof of something!

Mostly the up-and-comers are young,
not as young as I am, but still I fit in.
Fit in. Those words taste good.
Turns out, among artists
I actually might.

UNDERSTATED CROWD

Brandy's wearing a low-cut dress—
too low, slits up the side—
helmet-sprayed hair,
and the highest heels you can imagine.
The trying-so-hard look sticks out
in this understated, slick crowd.
Davy's wearing a thin tie, very hip.
My father's sporting a big smile.
He's got his arm around Davy.
One day not too long ago,
Davy and Dad disappeared into the library.
Davy emerged with a smile,
said he's glad Joe is his dad!
This shocker made me cry with relief.
He deserves a loving parent.
As Great-Aunt Dalvinka once said:
"Gay, shmay, who even cares?"

Around nine fifteen, Kiki and Ken stride in.
Kiki hugs Nastasia, spots me,
gives me a halfhearted little wave.
I almost fall over
with how sad that makes me feel.
I want to gallop over to her
and thank her for allowing me,
through her eyes, to discover who I am,
who I could become.
And for loving me.
Because I know she did.
My eyes keep finding Kiki.
She's wearing an electric-blue dress,

cobalt-blue suede shoes, and a magenta scarf;
she's as colorful as one of her paintings.
At one point she stands
in front of a small delicate collage
and doesn't budge.
There's thrumming in my gut,
which is saying,
"I want you to think I'm the most talented!"
Color me jealous!
I can tell myself I'm okay
'til I'm blue in the face,
but I want to hear it from her.
Is that sick?
On the other hand,
people are looking at my art!
Brandy wobbles over, drapes her arm
around my shoulder
as if she knows what I'm thinking.
In a way it's kind of touching
how hard she's trying.

There's wine and crackers on small plates.
Out of sheer nerves I gulp down
prodigious amounts of cheese.
I also chug down another two glasses of rosé.
I feel the giggles coming on,
but simultaneously
I think I might cry.
Laughing and crying
are laced mysteriously together.
I make sure I go for the giggles.

LAUGHING TOO LOUD

Around ten thirty
the gallery begins to thin out;
waiters start to remove the snacks.
Davy says Dad's ready to leave.
Dad winks, gives me the
"let's get out of here" look.
Nastasia whispers, "How do you feel?
Someone might *buy* your drawing!"
Nastasia's face is lit up like the North Star.
She smacks a wet kiss on my cheek,
says that I have to promise her to keep going.
When I turn, the feather in her hair
kind of zaps me in the eye.
This strikes me as hilarious.
I start to guffaw.
I'm laughing too loud,
and I don't seem to be stopping, either.
Cascades of pent-up emotion escape.
My voice climbs octaves in rabid hysteria.
At least I think those sounds
are coming out of me,
and from the way people are staring,
they probably are.
I'm bent over, gripping my stomach.
I shimmy near a wall trying to stabilize,
completely out of control.

COMMOTION

Meanwhile, there's a ruckus
at the front of the gallery.
Two people are pushing through others
who are leaving.
"That cab driver was a pill!
He got us lost forever!
I know this city better than he does,
but you kept saying to trust him.
Which is why we're *late*!"
says a girl emphatically.
"Well, you weren't exactly Vasco da Gama!"
says a guy, equally energized.
"If he'd gone across Seventy-Ninth Street,
we would've been here twenty minutes ago!"
says the girl.
These two are coming into full view.
They're young and glamorous.
The boy points: "There she is!"
It's Peter Collins!
He's gesturing at me!
This commotion belongs to Rachel!
"Sorry, sorry, excuse me,"
she says to everyone,
elbowing through the crowd.
"I didn't want to be late.
Well, not *this* late!" she tells onlookers.
I run toward her.
Her hair cascades all the way down to her waist.
She's even more gorgeous
than I remember.
I notice that she's peering at me.

Maybe smiling?
She's not trying to hide what her eyes
are almost shouting:
She's happy for me!

BORN ARTIST

"Rachel!"
"Don't get excited, Maisie, you snake.
I wasn't going to miss this, was I?
No! Of course not!
But I still hate you, you rotten-skunk-
of-a-boyfriend-stealing menace!"
"I *am* a rotten-skunk of a girl!"
I practically shout.
Peter Collins is holding on to Rachel
as if she's a helium balloon
that might blow away.
"You get to hate me," I splutter.
"But maybe you could hate me—
and also forgive me?"
"I'm not sure when
I'll stop hating you, Maisie,
but I figured maybe I could taper off slowly
and meanwhile see your oeuvre.
Wher*e is* it, anyway?"
I show her.
She doesn't say much for like
two or three years, it seems.
I don't inhale.
"Kiki's right about you, damn it!
You're a born artist!"
I hug her, and she lets me.

I think I'm crying again,
feeling so grateful
and also like such a rotten human being.
Is there anything better than being forgiven?
What's better than that?

DAYS TO COME

That night it takes me a long time to settle down
on the pull-out in my father's library.
Brandy explained, when she was making my bed,
that the leather-bound books with titles like
Remembrance of Things Past, The Pilgrim's Progress,
and *Martin Chuzzlewit* were only for show.
Behind them are *Peyton Place,*
Murder on the Orient Express, and
The Carpetbaggers, the books they actually read.
Brandy laughed: "I know! Pretentious, right?"
I'm learning about my father little by little.
It's been two hours since I got home, but I'm still restless,
so there are several trots around the apartment—
visits to the balcony
to gaze at the sky, which, because of the bright glow of Manhattan,
has stars I mostly cannot see.
I think of Richie in France.
Is he looking up, thinking of me?
"Bonsoir, ma copain."
Down below us, though,
are the barges
sluggishly moving up and down the East River.
This river connects to where I used to live.
But here, just a few miles south,
my brother and I are safe.

I incant this fact to myself, urgently, often,
because my body still clenches in fear
in random moments;
loud noises,
sudden movements
bring me back to the worst of my Parkchester days.
Davy still bangs his head sometimes.
But not tonight.
Over the Triborough Bridge come the first beams of light.
I hover in the kitchen,
have several snacks of crisp, salty pretzels
and the linzer torte my grandmother made for me
before I finally get drowsy.
Outside, the sky insists on brightening again,
so I stick my tired, dirty feet under the fresh covers
and finally descend into the pause
that separates one day
from the next better day.
And sure enough, I dream of the better days yet to come.

LIFE LONGING FOR ITSELF

I still listen to gloomy music,
like Billie Holiday's albums,
full of tortured yearnings;
songs that bleat over lost love.
Occasionally I feel as if I'm slipping down
into a dreary, misbegotten place,
with odd-looking characters,
stale coffee, mildewed furniture;
a room full of losers.
But most of the time,
I know that I don't belong there.
I belong in a paint-stained smock.
I have, despite everything,
or maybe because of it,
passion for this living of life.
My life means something,
because, no matter what's happened so far,
I am, as Gibran says,
a "living arrow . . . sent forth,"
a "daughter of Life's longing for itself."
I will "dwell in the house of tomorrow."
I am the pearl in the oyster.
I am; I just know I am.

AUTHOR'S NOTE

While this novel is fiction, it is greatly inspired by my own childhood.

I was born in the Bronx and lived there until the age of seven, when my father moved us to the suburbs. Even a dysfunctional family like mine with serious, sometimes even violent, troubles was not immune to the fantasy of a better life somewhere else, with our own backyard and barbecue.

But I decided to set this entire novel in the Bronx because it was, like my home, coming apart, in decline, and experiencing increased turbulence. For Maisie, the tense streets uptown create a growing, urgent need to escape, as mirrored by her impossible situation with her very disturbed parent.

I didn't so much write this story as let it pour out. In my own life, my relationship with my mother was defining, and it forced me to grow up a second time—through therapy, meditation, and travel—simply in order to survive. As in the novel, I did have a best friend whose mom was for her a challenge, but for me a lifesaver. I always thought that was an interesting dynamic in and of itself. Also, this is a sibling story. Maisie has to find a way to cherish her brother, Davy, rather than resent him. When she does, everything changes.

Whoever the "me" is that has lived on this earth for so long now, I recognize she was born with great determination. Although I bounced from career to career, location to location, boyfriend to boyfriend, and while very young had to spend time in a mental hospital, there was grit in my soul that sustained me. And, like Maisie, I was always an art girl. Art spoke to me as no human could. It allowed me to see other worlds and to feel deeply connected to them. It showed me there was a way to express the pulsing, intense, uncontainable feelings I had and to turn them into something

343

useful and lasting and even beautiful. Art sustained me and still does. I was lucky in this regard, and, as in this tale, the exposure came through my friend's mother who was herself a painter.

Despite everything, my own life has had some incredible moments. I got to live in Paris, learn French, study painting, and make lifelong friendships with incredible people. I worked with Jim Henson on award-winning animated films for television. I wrote prime-time sitcom, acted off Broadway with Sam Shepard and other amazing performers and playwrights, and debuted in London's West End. I shared students with Maurice Sendak at Parsons School of Design, where I was awarded a Distinguished Teachers Award. I reviewed children's books for the *New York Times* as well as drew editorial illustrations for the op-ed page. And I'm blessed to have remarkable, talented, supportive friends, students, and colleagues who inspire me daily. I've published with the help of brilliant, legendary agents and editors. I've performed my own work here in LA and in NYC as a Spoken Word artist, and traveled to India to further my own healing. I was fortunate to eventually marry a man, who, in many ways, is a twin soul, and who collaborated on several picture books.

So I offer this somewhat biographical but mostly fictional story in the tradition of the "wounded healer." We are legion. Part of the human legacy. One day, perhaps, we will collectively evolve and learn true kindness and it will be pervasive. Then we won't need to recount these poignant, troubling narratives. That would be a great thing.

Meanwhile, in this work, I am speaking heart-to-heart to anyone who relates. We never know who or what will rescue us, or how we will rescue ourselves . . .

Please note that to include certain cultural touchstones, I took some liberties with the timeline of events in this story.

ACKNOWLEDGMENTS

This story lived in me demanding to be heard, but early on, it only whispered incoherently. Back then, I had no idea there existed a poetic form—free verse—that would invite my deepest self to speak clearly, artfully, and directly. Fortunately, I discovered novels by Sonya Sones, Karen Hesse, Thalia Chaltas, and others. Once introduced to this narrative approach, my first draft rushed out nervously, quickly—and chaotically. This is the reason I have so many people to thank. I'd like to thank Lynzee Klingman for her lifelong friendship and for abiding with the family invasion that may have saved my life but certainly seeded this story.

My professional journey began when I was an illustrator. To the editors who spurred me on to write as well as draw books: Elaine Edelman, Robert Warren, Linda Zuckerman, you helped me dare to capture an entire new realm. And to my subsequent editors: Katherine Tegen, Nancy Siscoe, Neal Porter, Maria Modugno, Kathy Landwehr, Margaret Anastas, Valerie Garfield, Caitlyn Dlouhy, Arthur Levine, you are the best of the best.

To the sole writing teacher I studied with, the generous, brilliant John Rechy, who not only taught me everything but who also shared craft so eloquently that I came to eventually be able to teach others. And to Jay Levin, publisher of the *LA Weekly*, who printed my essays and interviews, which enabled me to have another sort of confidence. To Tom Shroder of *Tropic* magazine in the *Miami Herald*, who published my humorous nonfiction on the backside of Dave Barry's hilarious columns. And to Helen Gurley Brown, who personally edited my short stories for *Cosmopolitan*, which gave me another spring in my step. Lastly to my partners in feature films and TV writing, Arlene Sidaris, who was a perfect match for my sensibility and a joy to work with and Irv Wilson, with whom I could write hilarious and unforgettable first acts.

When this particular novel emerged, it was clear that I needed to find experts who would guide, challenge, and encourage me, so I thank Francoise Bui, Elana Golden, Karen Klockner, Lisa Levine, Bethany Strout, and Emma Dryden.

Of course, I must give much appreciation to my enduring sidekick, esteemed agent, and friend, Rick Richter, who is as honest to the bone as they come and as kind.

I am fortunate in my colleagues and fellow travelers who patiently, endlessly, benevolently offered me feedback, occasional praise, and vital advice: Kim Purcell, Susan Cuscuna, Carol Schlanger, Arlene Schindler, Roberto Loiederman, Kathleen Garrett, Melanie Chartoff, Leslie Hyatt, Ann Whitford Paul, Karen Winnick, Michelle Markel, Erica Silverman, and Carol Schwartz.

There were readers and pals who simply gave me reason to be hopeful: Susan Merson, Laura Valeri, April Wayland, Karen Dorr, Susan Dalsimer, Barney Saltzberg, Arlene Sarner, Truusje Kushner, Minju Chang, Joy Peskin, Nita Tucker.

I am grateful for the venues that invited me to perform excerpts from this work: Ronda Spinak's Jewish Women's Theater and Eve Brandstein's Poetry In Motion at Beyond Baroque.

For creating continuity and modeling their dedication, focus, and sharing in their talent, those who gather around my table twice a month: Jim Cox, Denise Doyen, Cami Gordon, Gail Israel, Hillary Perelyubskiy, Antoinette Portis, Michael Portis, and Beth Spiegel.

I am indebted for the time I spent in India on an ashram with fellow seekers who allowed me the peace of mind necessary to be able to listen to characters tell their tales. To C. J. Bigelow, Belinda Bauer, Doug Bentley, Skip Miller, and Rosie Shuster and to Sri Bhagavan and the monks who lifted so much darkness off me; my life and my pages are stronger because of you.

None of this would matter if it weren't for the keen eyes that belong to Erin Stein of Imprint, who embraced and understood this material and then suggested, in the most easily digested, non-fussy way, what rewrite would be needed to make the book viable, even when I thought I was "done." And to Nicole Otto, tireless human glue who kept me connected at Macmillan.

Lastly to my husband, Gerald, who deserves the most gratitude for living with someone who leads two lives, is moody, intense, bossy, confusing, and doesn't always agree to watch certain TV selections. You have always had a ridiculous, stalwart belief in me and my creative obsessions. Many decades ago on an early date, you sat in my living room reading a YA novel I'd published—too ensconced in it to want to chat with me. I took umbrage until you pointed out that I was jealous of *myself*! You've been my friend, my fan, my honey, and that is why, despite these words, there are no words that can express my sincere belief that with you, I hit the jackpot.

RESOURCES

The National Domestic Violence Hotline

Operating around-the-clock, seven days a week, confidential, and free of cost, the National Domestic Violence Hotline provides life-saving tools and immediate support to enable victims to find safety and live free of abuse.

thehotline.org
1-800-799-SAFE (7233)

National Suicide Prevention Lifeline

If you are afraid that you might hurt yourself or are feeling suicidal, the National Suicide Prevention Lifeline provides 24/7 free, confidential support over the phone and online.

suicidepreventionlifeline.org
1-800-273-8255

National Runaway Safeline

The Runaway Safeline is a free, confidential hotline and online chat service available 24/7 that provides guidance for youth who have run away, are considering running away, or are homeless.

1800runaway.org
1-800-RUNAWAY (786-2929)

SafeHorizon

SafeHorizon provides 24/7 free, confidential counseling and support to survivors of domestic violence and abuse in both English and Spanish.

safehorizon.org
1-800-621-HOPE (4673)

SAMHSA's National Helpline

SAMHSA's National Helpline is a confidential, free, 24-hours-a-day, 365-days-a-year information service, in English and Spanish, for individuals and family members facing mental and/or substance use disorders. This service provides referrals to local treatment facilities, support groups, and community-based organizations.

samhsa.gov
1-800-662-HELP (4357)

Crisis Text Line

Crisis Text Line provides free, confidential crisis intervention via text message. Text HOME to 741741 from anywhere in the United States, anytime, about any type of crisis, and a live, trained crisis counselor will help you handle the situation.

crisistextline.org
Text HOME to 741741